The Leopard's Reward

Short Stories

Gerard Loughran

First published 2017 by IRON Press
5 Marden Terrace
Cullercoats
North Shields
NE30 4PD
tel/fax +44(0)191 2531901
ironpress@blueyonder.co.uk
www.ironpress.co.uk

ISBN 978-0-9954579-0-4
Printed by imprintdigital.com

Cover and book Design Brian Grogan and Peter Mortimer
Leopard drawing © John Johnston
< www.jwjonline.net>

Typeset in Minion Pro

IRON Press books are distributed by NBN International
and represented by Inpress Ltd
Churchill House, 12 Mosley Street,
Newcastle upon Tyne, NE1 1DE
tel: +44(0)191 2308104
www.inpressbooks.co.uk

Gerard Loughran

Born and educated in Newcastle upon Tyne, Gerard Loughran embarked on a 48-year career in journalism as a 17-year-old junior reporter for *The Northern Echo.* After editing duties with the *Newcastle Evening Chronicle,* he moved abroad and spent the remainder of his 48-year-career in Africa, the Middle East and Europe. This included more than a dozen years in senior editorial capacities for the *Daily Nation* of Kenya, and 18 years as a foreign correspondent for the American news agency, *United Press International.*

For UPI, Loughran was successively bureau chief in Beirut, Paris and Moscow, covering the rise of the Palestinian guerrilla movements (and being taken hostage by one of them), the Yom Kippur war, Vietnam peace negotiations in the French capital and the stirrings of anti-Soviet dissent in the fading years of Leonid Brezhnev. In 1976, he was appointed head of international news in New York.

Six years later, Loughran accepted an invitation from the Aga Khan, founder and principal shareholder of the Nation group of newspapers, to return to Europe and establish a service providing news of the little-reported developing nations. *Compass News Features* operated from Luxembourg and later London. Prior to retirement, Loughran wrote a history of the Nation group to mark its 50th anniversary in 2010. *Birth of a Nation* was widely hailed as an honest and accurate assessment of the newspapers and the nation of Kenya, both born in the same year.

Acknowledgments

Grateful thanks are due to my sister and brother, Pat and John, and to two former UPI colleagues, Alex Frere and Ray Moseley, who read all of these stories before publication and responded in usefully critical but supportive terms. And importantly to my good friend, Harris Dousemetzis, who heard many of the yarns merely as anecdotes, but pressed me to commit them to print.

The Stories

About These Stories

It is obvious that anyone who spent nearly fifty years living, writing and reporting abroad must have heard a million strange stories and collected bizarre experiences of his own that would make good listening back home with the telly off and the blinds drawn. My problem was that as a journalist trained in the old school of unremittingly objective reporting, the notion of nudging events in a certain direction, applying gloss here and spin there, solving a problem by guesswork, in other words *writing fiction,* was hard to contemplate. But then, I thought, I'm not pretending it is true. These are just stories.

And so incidents I was involved in, tales people told me, fragments of conversation began appearing on my computer screen in lightly imagined form. For instance, *The Dire Prophecy of Seaman Flack* is based on a frightening experience, one I have never been able to explain, from my early days as a sub-editor in the north of England.

The Christmas Party owes much to a still-unsolved mystery in the street where I now live, and *A Change of Shifts* contains elements from my late father's experience in a real-life mining disaster.

The title story, *The Leopard's Reward,* was told to me by a Kenyan photographer who heard it from his uncle, who swore it happened to him. It has to be said, however, that any time I mention it to another African, I get a slow, negative shake of the head. *Time to Go* is also from my favourite continent. We never learn the full name of Pinky, but he is a synthesis of a vanished breed, the white man who loved Africa so much, at least the Africa that he first encountered, that he could not bear to leave it, whatever the cost.

Other stories have no direct starting point in my life or experiences, but I just have to listen to a conversation on a crowded bus or eavesdrop in a local tea-room to spot the feisty old lady who took on the supermarkets, the poison-pen writer who lost her daughter's love and the young man whose bravado camouflaged a life of fear and failure.

If everything I have written did not happen, then it could. In this sense, there is no such thing as fiction.

Gerard Loughran
November 2017

The Leopard's Reward

I KNOW WE BLACK FOLKS HAVE OUR WITCHY STORIES, TALES TO frighten the children or bolster the courage of our elders in hard times, which alas have been many. But I am a modern African. I have a bachelor's degree from a recognised university and I know that God does not reside at the summit of Mount Kenya. I work on my country's biggest newspaper and what I am about to tell you is true.

At holiday times, it is customary for our working people to leave the cities and return to their villages to be with families, to feast, to remember, and to slip something small to their country cousins. Accordingly, I left the capital a few days before Christmas and took a bus back to my home area near the Lake. A few seats behind me were two age-mates, so naturally upon arrival we headed for the Bristol Hotel, actually a shack of cardboard and corrugated iron, where we sat on beer crates, slowly emptying their contents over the course of the evening while consuming plates of *githeri*, rice and goat's meat.

Let me state right away that the beer did not induce or distort in any way the experience which took place as I walked the last mile to my family home in the pre-midnight hour. What I saw, I saw. What happened, happened.

At first, I thought it was a blanket roll in the middle of the dirt road, fallen off a bus roof perhaps. Then it moved, and by shafts of moonlight through the trees, I saw the rosettes on the pelt, the lithe, powerful body, and the massive skull turned directly towards me. A leopard! I was a dead man.

Some white people have romantic notions about Africans and wild animals, that we maintain a kind of spiritual affinity with them, that our closeness to the earth makes us one under the skin, noble Brother Lion, clever Sister Serpent and so on. I would hesitate to characterise this thinking as racist but certainly it is nonsense. Wild animals scare us to death, they terrorise our villages, destroy our crops and sometimes steal our children. Our view is that non-domestic animals should be killed without question and if edible, promptly devoured.

Right now, however, it looked as if I was the one facing such a fate. Mentally, I measured the distance between where I stood and my mother's front door. Given a leopard's ability to cover ground at 36 miles per hour, I would be dead meat between its powerful jaws before I got halfway. Cautiously, I took a step backward whereupon the animal rose, a female, more than two feet at the shoulder, five feet nose to tail, maybe forty kilos. Instantly, I froze. She stared at me intently. Why had she not attacked? Why was I not dead already?

The guidebooks all refer to big cats "coughing." The one before me was not coughing, she was making a strange, impacted, mewling noise. She was also distractedly tossing her huge head from side to side like a fly-tormented horse, while between her front paws were pooled what seemed to be lakes of saliva. Strangest of all, her jaws were wide apart in a huge gape, as if she was emitting a furious, silent roar – and now I realised they had been that way since our encounter began. The truth dawned on me. This animal could not close her mouth.

Moonlight turns everything black and silver. But I know that the eyes watching me were leopard-yellow, the huge, curving fangs stained the colour of old ivory, and the glossy saliva dripping from her bottom jaw streaked blood red.

The leopard took a pace towards me and I backed away. But then she lifted her head, side-on against the moon, the gaping jaws outlined in profile, and I saw the extra fang. Not curved, not a top jaw tooth nor a bottom one, but something dark and slender, extending from the roof of the leopard's mouth to the tongue below. She had somehow picked up a foreign object, which was lodged between her jaws, preventing the leopard from closing her mouth.

The obvious solution was to call the Game Department, but this was before the days of mobile phones. The Bristol Hotel had a telephone but

I knew without question that the leopard would not allow me to retrace my steps and even if she did, she would drown in her own body fluids by the time help arrived.

Looking straight at me, she slowly sank to the ground, turned her head again and lifted it towards the moon. There was no doubt I was being invited to intervene, to use my human intelligence to put an end to this animal's hideous suffering. The invitation was clear and my human intelligence set out my next step. It was human courage, or rather the lack of it, that was holding me back. For what I was being required to do was *put my hand into the mouth of a wild leopard.*

It was the grunting, helpless, choking sounds which finally propelled me forward. She did not move. I craned to see better. Was it a thorn twig, a tough piece of acacia, part of a game trap, a nail even? I went down on two knees, praying hard to the god I knew did not live atop Mount Kenya, shuffled forward and reached out my hand. In seconds I will have only one arm, I thought. In minutes I will be dead. Carefully, the leopard turned her head, facilitating my movements. I reached inside. Smooth, slimy, pencil-thin, jointed, it was a bone, a dik-dik's maybe, or a Tommy gazelle's, from the leopard's last meal, lodged painfully, a sort of victim's revenge.

My touch on the bone was light but the leopard jerked in pain. The jaws were as far apart as they could go. To ease the bone out, I would first have to press one end deeper into the flesh, into the roof of the mouth or down into the tongue. I shuddered at the thought. Was there a less painful way? I could feel her lower teeth scrape my wrist and the leopard's foetid breath billowed hot and steamy into my face as its saliva streamed across my knuckles.

I have always had strong fingers, my farming family's bequest to me. Adjusting my kneeling position, I braced my index and middle fingers round the back of the bone and pressed hard against the joint with my thumb. Instantly, it cracked in half and the two pieces fell into my palm. Cautiously, I withdrew my hand, got to my feet and backed off. Ignoring me, the leopard exultantly emitted that growling, rumbling, un-lion-like leopard's roar it had been prevented from making for who knows how long. It raised its head and shook it vigorously from side to side, sending sheets of bloodied saliva across the *murram* road, into the grassy edges and over my shoes.

I knew at that point that I was quite safe and we looked at each other steadily for an age. The leopard gulped and swallowed many times, then, breathing normally again and without ceremony, she turned, bounded from the road and vanished into the bush.

It was long after I had greeted the family, eaten yet more meat and downed gallons of hot, sweet tea that I remembered the cameras that had been round my neck throughout the episode. How could the Photographer of the Year three years running fail to record one of the most extraordinary animal sequences of all time? But, truth to tell, I was not dismayed. It had been a private encounter, a unique interaction between the species. Perhaps it was for that reason that I have never, until now, told this story, nor its extraordinary conclusion.

When my mother opened our front door the next morning, what she found lying across the doorstep was the carcase of a freshly killed Thomson's gazelle. It had not been trapped or shot, it had been suffocated in the style of a leopard. The teeth marks were still visible around its clenched windpipe.

The family, if ever the subject comes up, still puzzle about this strange episode, about how this kill appeared on the doorstep between midnight and dawn. They are not to know, of course, that it was not chance, some gazelle which escaped a leopard's clutches to die randomly at our door, that it was in fact a gift, the leopard's reward.

Letters to Write, Traps to Lay...

Dear Sirs,

You will doubtless perceive similarities between this letter and complaints which this organisation has delivered to you over the past many months, letters which you have very possibly (and if so, unwisely) consigned to your rubbish bins.

To refresh your memories, let us briefly set out our areas of concern:

Minor:
1. Packaging which is wasteful, excessive and difficult for older people.
2. Ill-designed items, such as circular medicinal tablets which roll away when dropped, or items which are designed for visual appeal, e.g. perfectly round, perfectly red and perfectly tasteless tomatoes.
3. Discount selling which ignores the needs of single customers unable to consume a large item in the time period recommended.
4. Your continued provision of free plastic bags harmful to the environment.
5. Your failure to deny entry to women who go shopping in daylight whilst clad in night attire.

Major:
1. Purchasing policies which force down the prices you pay suppliers to an unrealistic level, pressuring some dairy farmers, for example, out of business.
2. Your ruthless acquisition of sites for retail outlets which destroy small business already in the area.

3. Your use of overseas producers whose employees are forced to work in inhumane conditions.

Our complaints demanded remedial action, but regrettably this has not taken place. Nor has the necessary statement of contrition and undertaking of reform appeared in the Personal columns of The Times newspaper. Thus a decision has been taken at the highest level to proceed with actions which will seriously embarrass your retailing organisation in terms of reputation and profit, as well as inflicting injuries of a nature we do not wish to specify upon individual officers of your company.

We trust the deadly serious action campaign we have now launched will result in a hasty reappraisal of our requests.

(Signed) Warriors for a Better World.

'And there we go, Trixie,' said the typist, whisking the letter from her battered portable, 'that will give them something to think about, will it not?' Trixie's chihuahua eyes signalled agreement from the comfort of her basket. The old lady smoothed rubber gloves over her bejewelled fingers, folded the letter into three and slipped it into an envelope already stamped and addressed to corporate headquarters. Then she added it to a large pile by her typewriter.

'Is everything there, Trixie? Letters to the retail outlets containing white powder. It's just powder, but what will the managers think when they open their mail, my darling? They will think why, what have we here? Flour, perhaps, or bicarbonate of soda? Looks a bit like salt or sugar, but they won't dare taste it. After all, it could be something nastier, something toxic maybe, arsenic, anthrax, rat poison, who's to tell? They won't be too happy to get their unsolicited gifts, Trixie, will they?

'Probably the other managers won't either, the ones who don't get the powder but get cheap rubber gloves instead, a pair apiece. They are perfectly new gloves so they should be grateful, but we don't think they will. Some of the fingertips will be stained red and certainly they will wonder what that red could be. Surely, being surgical gloves, they will think of blood first, won't they, my love? But it might not be blood or even if it is blood it might not be, well, tainted. And it could just as easily be raspberry jam. Oh, what a conundrum they will face!'

* * * * *

The Warrior for a Better World rose early. 'Wake up Trixie, dear, we have a busy day ahead of us. Have the letters had their effect, we wonder? Five days now, time enough for them to panic, don't you agree? But first, our weapons for today.' She surveyed the kitchen counter. 'Needles. Useful things needles, aren't they Trix, quite unobtrusive. Slip them into takeaway meals, Italian or Indian or good old English cottage pies, no bother at all and nobody will ever notice, at least not until the customer tries to eat his supper and then there will be trouble. Also, a little pair of nail scissors for my pocket. Now they are really handy, you can snip open half a dozen packets of frozen foods in seconds with these scissors and nobody the wiser. Not that half a dozen spoiled meals will bankrupt these fellows but after the warnings they will be getting from head office, they are going to be so nervous they will have to throw out whole freezers full and they won't like that, not a bit.'

She rummaged in a cupboard, then finally: 'Ah, here they are, five sterile hypodermic syringes for one pound fifty. That's a bargain, is it not, little one? Dirty them up a bit, half-fill them with something nasty-looking and leave them lying about. Whoever discovers them, some innocent shelf-stacker, will be hysterical, poor thing, and just imagine the chaos. Not that it's his fault, is it, Trixie? But somebody has to suffer until they see sense.'

The old lady took a plastic bag and carefully filled it with her weapons. 'Come on, darling, let's go, we have a busy day ahead of us, so many things to do… actions to take, traps to lay.' The chihuahua, scrambled out of its corner and waited for the click of the lead on its collar.

* * * * *

Unusually, there were two uniformed security officers at the entrance to the shopping mall. 'Excuse me, madam,' said the first formally, holding out his hand for the bag.

'Excuse me? What do you mean?' the old lady demanded.

'Your bag, please, madam, we need to examine it, special security.'

'Special security! Young man, I am not a shoplifter. You may not have noticed, but I am walking INTO the mall, I am not running AWAY!'

By now the plastic loops were twisted around Trixie's leash. Shoppers were turning to watch.

'Madam,' wearily, 'it's only precautionary...'

The security man stopped suddenly and the old lady turned.

'Why officer!' she exclaimed. 'How lovely to see you!'

'Oh, it's you, Miss Perkins.' PC Wright smiled, strolling up to the pair. 'Didn't recognise you there, bit of a flap on this morning.' He nodded to the security man, who turned away.

'They wanted to examine my bag! Can you imagine!'

'Just a precaution, Miss Perkins, they have their job to do. But it's fine, do go on, the store is busy today.'

Miss Perkins smiled, 'So kind of you, officer.' She tied Trixie to the dog rail then turned and waved to the watching constable before merging with the milling crowds of shoppers.

* * * * *

PC Wright was still on duty an hour later when the old lady emerged, untied her dog and dropped her empty plastic bag into the rubbish bin at the entrance.

'Ticked everything off your list, Miss Perkins?' the policeman enquired.

'Indeed I have, officer, all done, mission accomplished! But I must confess I am rather concerned.'

'How is that, Madam?'

'Well, there were men there, in the aisles and at all the entrances, who looked very ... I don't know, threatening. Not a smile from any of them. And there were a lot of... I think they were store detectives, many more than usual. It quite put me off and I took much longer than usual to do... the things I had to do. Is there some problem, do you know?'

'Nothing you should worry about, Miss Perkins.' He bent forward, confidentially. 'Just between us two – and that's also why I'm here – they've had a serious warning from head office to be on their guard. Seems some crazy person has been bombarding them with threatening letters, so they are all a bit nervous today.'

'Good gracious, Constable, what are they expecting to happen?'

The policeman chortled: 'Nuclear war, you would think from the briefing I got!'

'Oh dear, how silly!'

They chuckled together, then Miss Perkins said: 'Well, thank you, officer, and now we must be off. Come, Trixie, we have lots to do...' She moved out of earshot '... letters to write, traps to lay...'

The Dire Prophecy of Seaman Flack

THE LINED FOOLSCAP SHEETS WERE YELLOW AT THE EDGES AND THE writing was faded but legible. The paper was stapled in three lots, headed *SESSIONS I, II, III* and dated September 19, 20, 21, 1955. I read from the top sheet: "Present: Mr Schofield, Alan, Frank, Jerry, Maureen." And suddenly I remembered – it was that spook business we got into, three nights with the alphabet and the glass tumbler, nights that fascinated and finally terrified us.

There was always a dead hour after midnight for the sub-editors on our provincial daily. Last copy had gone down but we could not leave until 1 a.m. Usually the cards came out but that night we just smoked and chatted, feet up on the desks. How we got onto the Hereafter I do not remember, but Maurice Schofield said he had done it before and had achieved remarkable results. And our chief sub-editor was a serious man. He said you didn't need an Ouija board with a pointer that people joked about, just the letters of the alphabet in a circle and an upturned glass in the middle. The late-shift copy-taker was Maureen – on the *Echo* the telephone girls were well-bred young ladies hoping to advance to secretarial positions – and she obligingly scissored A to Z and 1 to 9 from a paper offcut and agreed to sit outside the circle and take notes. Not that we expected anything to happen, it was all too absurd for words.

I had found the transcripts in a carton now at my feet marked 'The Echo Years' from my days on that paper. I winced, how pompous! There were Royal Society of Arts test papers in Government and Economics, notebooks filled with early, clumsy shorthand, a textbook on law for journalists and a framed award in my name, a Certificate of Proficiency in Journalism. A long-expired trade union card had a jokey drawing of a head where the member's photo should be and there was a packet of stained and bent greetings cards from my mates – "To Jerry on your 20th birthday, Good luck, pal." Mostly they were of a comic nature about beer and busty women, though there was also an expensive, be-ribboned card, "To a Loving Son from Mam and Dad."

A pink folder held a letter of appointment as a trainee reporter at twenty-eight shillings per week; a five-year apprenticeship contract – red-tape-bound, Gothic-scripted and entitled "Articles of Agreement"; a letter of commendation from the Editor with an eight-shillings-per-week pay increase, and an instruction to transfer from district office to head office, from reporter to sub-editor.

That I was sitting here knee-deep amongst these fragments of my past was due to my wife, Marjorie. I had, she pointed out, concluded a long and successful career in journalism (or "the media" as she modishly called it, an expression I try to avoid). I had played roles of some importance in great national events across more than half a century, I had known the great and, if not the good, then the powerful, I had been honoured by the monarch and I was privy to secrets that perhaps now could be brought into the light. In other words, it was time to write my memoirs. She even had a title: *JEREMIAH BANKS: Fifty Years Before the Masthead.*

I wasn't sure about Marjorie's title (who knew about sailing before the mast these days, or indeed what a masthead was?) but I could see her point. The first two years in our rural retirement home had been exciting – planning and supervising extensions to the cottage, landscaping our six acres and the fine stand of Scots pines, plus frequent expenses-paid trips to conferences and seminars in London and overseas where the opinions of a respected retired editor were welcomed. Except after a while, the invitations slowed. The new breed of electronics-oriented media men (sometimes I have to use the M word!) were now in charge and newspapers became vehicles of infotainment which I could no longer recognise. Eventually, the letters and the phone calls stopped coming– just occasionally a book to review, a polite request to meet with a Ph.D. student, even once, sadly, a vicar's invitation to open a garden fête where nobody knew who or what I was. At least Marjorie knew: I was a dinosaur!

'Take a long holiday somewhere,' she said. 'Money is not a problem. Go on your own, take all those boxes of yours, work at your own pace, write your book. You did some fine things. They deserve to be recorded.'

So here I was on a luxury cruise, not yet writing but researching sporadically, recovering memories, occasionally astonished, more often puzzled by events half a century old. The chummy *Echo* years were good ones for us young men – discovering the true range of our talents, enjoying our comradeship in relative poverty, stingy landladies, countless cigarettes, expending excess energy by jumping over pillar boxes upon our 1 a.m. release into the darkened streets. Alan Thompson nearly always won those competitions. He was spry, sinewy, restless, crew-cut (to the Editor's distaste) and a Londoner – to our distaste until his quirky, generous personality won us over.

The last I recall of him before we all split up for National Service or moved to other jobs was a letter from Canada. Alan had gone to work in some distant silver mine. One sentence stuck in my mind: "We never sleep on Saturdays until the last beer crate has been emptied and the last waitress laid." I suppose I remembered because his life was so excitingly different to mine, where laying waitresses was rarely on the agenda.

Now, on an impulse, I Googled his name, guiltily conscious that I had never made much effort to keep in touch with the old gang. None had achieved my eminence in the industry though back then several had been my equals, if not my betters. I had moved early into foreign reporting and links were geographically broken, not my fault, I reasoned.

Alan's very common moniker produced 13.3 million results. I refined my search, using such autobiographical facts as I could recall, and suddenly, shockingly, it was there: "Alan Thompson (1934-1958)." The report was fragmentary, from the archives of a long-folded Alaskan newspaper, but it referred to his London (Dulwich) origins and journalistic work in the north of England. After the silver mine, he had worked on small newspapers in Canada and North America before signing on as a trawler hand fishing for king crabs in the Bering Sea. Unusually foul weather blew up, and his vessel, *Country King*, managed to transmit a single radio message reporting serious icing-up. An empty life raft was discovered 10 days later. The trawler and its 20-strong crew were never found. Alan's name was 20th on the official death toll.

I was stunned. Not so much that he was dead at 24, more that he had been dead so long. My mind wandered back. Maurice Schofield, dead, too, of course – our boss, our talented, highly-strung CSE. There had been a *Press Gazette* obit, I remembered, killed by a stroke in retirement. Still, he was a generation older than the rest of us. But also dead, quite recently, my best friend from that time, Frank Arthurs, as I had learned from his widow only a few months after we corresponded for the first time in years. Frank, aged 76, cancer. He knew when he wrote, of course, which is probably why he interrupted our long silence, a farewell really.

* * * * *

Maurice's clipped, bossy tones came back to my mind like yesterday. At his instruction, we placed our fingertips lightly on the upturned glass and the giggling subsided. But when he raised his head and with immense solemnity inquired, 'Is anybody there?' a roar of laughter went up and we nearly broke up on the spot. How I wish we had! But Maurice was unamused and this feisty little man was not to be crossed. Either be serious or we all go home, he demanded. So we put our fingers back, suppressing our giggles, and Maurice sought again and again to raise the dead.

Most of us were wearily supporting our right arms on our left elbows when the glass twitched. I looked directly across at Alan. He appeared startled. It was not so much *movement,* it was as if energy had invaded the glass. Maurice asked again: 'Is anybody there?' This time the glass did move. Slowly, painfully almost, it left the centre of the circle and dragged across the desk, searching, it seemed, among the ring of letters before heading towards Y. With what seemed like growing energy, it backtracked to E, then finally S. YES.

Maurice apart, we were dumbstruck, our fingertips still on the tumbler. No-one said anything, but one thought was uppermost in all our minds: this could not be true, so who was pushing the glass? I was only certain about one thing: it was not me.

I check Maureen's ancient script for that very first dialogue.

Who are you? ROBERTMANNERS

How did you die? PLAGUE

What year? 1348

Where? MELCOMBE

The silence was intense. Maureen, pale under her dark hair, a row of pens laid out before her, stared at her pad. We looked at Maurice. He went on:
Did many die?
ITSINTHEHISTORYBOOKS
Did you have a family? WIFEANDFIVE
Did they die, too? FORJESUSSAKE

We looked at each other. Was that anger, an exclamation of impatience, or was it a prayer?

Where are you now?
The glass remained immobile, not a tremor under our fingers.
Are you happy?
Silence.
Can we help you?
Nothing.

The glass felt dead, inert. Robert Manners had gone. We rested our arms. 'They don't like being asked that question,' Maurice said, 'about where they are. I shouldn't have raised it.' The rest of us were looking at each other. Frank held up his hand: 'I absolutely swear I was not pushing the glass.' 'Nor me, nor me,' from everybody. 'How about pulling it?' someone asked. Couldn't be done, we all agreed. It would tip over.
We were keen to go again. Once more the glass came to life.
Who are you? SUSIE
How did you die? UNDERANOMNIBUS
When did…? TOOMUCHCHAMPAGNEDANCINGINSTREETSO-GAYDANCINGWITHOURBEAUX

This was the longest single sentence we had yet received and the glass seemed to gather speed, or maybe knowledge of where the letters were positioned.

What year…? IWASALWAYSTHECHATTYONEANDTHEPRETTI-ESTEVERYONESAIDSO

And abruptly, chatty, pretty, gabbling Susie left us. The glass just sat there. 'What happened?' somebody asked, startled. 'You mean now or then?' said Maurice. *Now,* was the question in my own mind. Where did she go and why? Was there an authority, a time-limit, a rota, God help us a queue, out there, up there? Maurice addressed the *then*. 'I think she may have been a flapper, a debutante in the 1920s, out dancing in some Mayfair street, drunk on champagne. And beaux, meaning boyfriends, nobody uses that word now. Nor omnibus, either.'

Beaux had caused problems for Maureen. Indeed making sense of the glass's literary output was difficult. There were no punctuation signs; we whispered the letters as the glass touched them and Maureen tried to separate them into words, racing to keep pace with the glass. Thus she had, 'Too much champagne, dancing in street, so gay – dancing with our beaux.' And, 'I was always the chatty one, and the prettiest, everyone said so.'

We were excited, desperate for a third contact, but it was after 2 am and Maurice, long-married and a creature of habit, said we could try again tomorrow night. Meanwhile, why not learn a bit more about the plague and the Charleston?

* * * * *

Twelve hours later, over lunchtime beers in the Golden Fleece, three of us met to discuss the bizarre events of early that morning. The nervy jokiness quieted as Alan reported on the researches we had asked him to make in the town library: 'In two years, the Black Death, a form of bubonic plague, swept like a forest fire from China through Europe and into mediaeval England, killing 1.5 million of this country's total population, then estimated at 4 million. The disease was carried aboard merchant ships by flea-ridden rats and first made landfall in southwest England, probably Bristol.'

I remember Alan looking up from his notebook and asking, 'So when…?' We looked blank. He answered himself: 'Thirteen hundred and forty-eight... and where?' By then we had guessed. Melcombe? 'Correct, then known as Melcombe Regis in the county of Dorset. The home town of Robert Manners.'

There was either nothing to say or too much. Eventually, somebody mentioned Susie. Alan's investigations into the flapper era were less successful but contemporary reports said that night-time dancing in the streets of London's West End by bright young things awash with champagne was a regular occurrence. An accident with an omnibus seemed not only possible but inevitable.

We sipped our pints in the familiar back room of our favourite pub, trying to come to terms with this thing. Sure, any one of us could have been to the library, just like Alan, and mugged up about the plague and Melcombe to bluff our mates. But the session had happened spontaneously, entirely unplanned, and we were not history buffs or academics who would carry such dates and names in our heads. With Susie, maybe it was different. The flapper period was not so long ago and an imaginative reporter could dream up a yarn of equal vagueness. Still, both stories sounded convincing. As for the glass, somebody HAD to be pushing it, we agreed. But one by one, we solemnly raised a hand and declared our innocence. Even if one of us pushed, the letters were in a circle and while that person could possibly guide the glass away from him or to his right or left, he could not pull it forward without it tipping over. Alan suggested that the glass seemed to move better when Frank placed his finger on it, something I had noticed without its really registering. 'What do you mean,' Frank said sharply, 'we touch it together!' Which was not quite true, there was no military precision involved and when Frank's finger came on, I could swear the thing came vividly to life. We looked at him. 'Well,' he said slowly, 'my grandmother was a medium, they said she had the gift.'

* * * * *

Maureen prepared a new, improved version of the letters ring, with YES and NO as complete words, plus an ampersand, a period and a comma. She looked less nervous than last night but refused emphatically when somebody suggested she might like to take a turn on the glass. This time there was no laughing when Maurice demanded: 'Is anybody there?'

It took about five minutes. The glass slid directly to YES.

Who are you? BAGGYTHEYCALLUSGEORDIELAD

You're a Geordie? What happened to you? KILLEDINTHEMONTY-WITHMEMATE

Sorry, killed what…?

('Nineteen-twenty-five,' hissed Frank, startling us all. 'Montagu pit disaster, Scotswood on Tyne.')

The glass moved: 1925MONTYPIT38MEN&BOYSWATERFROMT

HEPARADISEDROWNEDORGASSED

(Frank whispered to Maurice: 'Get his full name, we can check the death toll.')

But the glass went on: NOTNICEFUCKINGDYINGUNDER-GROUND

Maybe it was the shock of the swear word, but Maurice broke his own rule: *Can we reach you somewhere, help you?*

Immediately, the glass died.

'What have we got?' Maurice asked briskly, taking charge but flustered by the F-word, glancing sideways, apologetically, at Maureen. Alan huddled with her, slashing pen marks between her letters, making words.

'What we've got is a Geordie lad nicknamed Baggy who was drowned in a pit disaster in 1925 with his mate. It seems there were 38 men and boys, all dead, I suppose. He says it was not a nice experience. I think he's in Paradise.'

Frank broke in testily: 'Not Paradise, not Heaven… he means Paradise Pit, it was next to the Montagu, a sealed off coalmine, worked out, abandoned. Somebody put a charge or a pick in the wrong place and broke through into the old seams. Foul water and black damp poured into the Monty. Miners near the inrush didn't have a chance.' He looked up and explained: 'That's where we come from, my family, Newcastle. My father and grandfather were both on that shift but far away from the break and they got out. Everybody knows the story, my dad knew all the dead. A pity you didn't get his name, Maurice. 'Baggy' doesn't tell us much.'

Maurice ignored this remark and suggested the spirit's claims would be easy to check in the newspaper archives. Frank was dismissive. 'There's nothing to check. What he said is perfectly correct.' In the silence that followed I wondered why we were all getting so tense, what was this experience doing to us? I suggested we move on, fingers back on the glass.

Peter Smith, aged 14 (TRIEDTOREACHAGULLSNESTBUTFEL-

LOFFTHECLIFF); Jane, a serving girl from Yorkshire (ITHINKI-COUGHEDANDCOUGHEDMYWHOLELIFE); Reverend Edmonds from a poor parish in Worcestershire (IWASPHYSICIANMORETH-ANPRIESTTHEIRDISEASESKILLEDMEFINALLY). An old lady, no name, came and went (YOUARENOTWISETODOTHIS).

Finally there was Seaman Flack, dreadful Seaman Flack. With a wavelet of distantly remembered fear, I checked through the transcript:

What happened to you? BOMBEDNORTHATLANTIC1942

What was your ship? CITYOFBUNOSARESS

City of Buenos Aires? YOUTHINKIMLYING

No, no… was it a warship? BLOODYKIDSGOINGTOAMERICA

Out of where? LIVERPOOLOFCOURSE

Were the crew British? STINKINGLASCARS

What was your job? WHAT

Your position, rank? SIGNALMAN

Who was your Master? FUCKINGQUESTIONSKEEPOUTJUST-FUCKINGKEEPOUTJUST

Shocked as we realised what the glass was spelling out, instinctively we lifted our fingers and it stopped moving immediately. Moments later, it was clearly inanimate.

Maurice turned to Maureen, who was near tears. 'I'm terribly sorry about that, the anger and, er, the language. It wasn't us.' He looked around. 'I think that's enough for tonight.'

* * * * *

It was a subdued huddle next day in the Fleece. We no longer debated if one of us was cheating. At times, the glass became so alive, so apparently eager to move that it squirmed under our fingers, twisting on the spot in a way that no fingertip could engineer. More disturbing was the language. None of us in 1955 would dream of using the F-word in front of a girl. To require Maureen to write down swear words letter by letter was simply beyond us.

So were we genuinely in contact with the spirit world and if so, why? 'It's so pointless,' complained Frank. 'Nothing happens, we get nowhere… a few short sentences, some information about the past which we confirm in the library next day, then what?'

That became the focal question: Why did they communicate with us?

We had all read mystery stories which talked about the release of restless spirits. There was none of that, just inconsequential, aimless facts. They did not ask for anything. They did not reveal anything. They did not look into the future ('or tell us who will win the Grand National,' interpolated Alan). Most exasperating, they did not stay, they shut down (or *were* shut down) the moment reference was made to their present state.

It was Frank who expressed the fear growing in our minds: 'Can they harm us?' Then, 'For God's sake, how could they! But they do seem to be getting nastier. Flack is evil. And remember what the old lady said, *You're not wise to do this.*'

We wondered, should we call it a day? As rational young men, we did not want to admit we were scared of phantoms. We were also curious, we wanted answers.

Alan particularly seemed disturbed by Flack and we decided he should replace Maurice as the question master tonight and that whatever happened, this session would be the last.

* * * * *

All these years later, my memory of that final meeting with the spirits was deficient in specifics but vivid with emotions. And the dominant one was fear. I reached for the final transcript. Alan started.

Is Seaman Flack there? Seaman Flack? Mr Flack will you speak to us?

The glass stayed dead.

Mr Flack, we mean no harm, we are interested in your experiences.

The tumbler jerked, receiving that unique energy charge we had come to recognise, then revolved steadily.

Mr Flack, thank you. You were on the City of Buenos Aires when it was bombed in 1942? YES

You said you were a signalman? YESYESYESCHRISTSAKE

Mr Flack, why are you lying to us?

The glass remained immobile, but pulsing, alive. We tensed, looking at Alan.

Mr Flack, there was no such vessel as the City of Buenos Aires. There was a City of Benares, but it was torpedoed, not bombed, and that was 1940 not 1942. It was carrying child evacuees from England but they were going to Canada not America. Seventy-seven kids lost along with 121 crew members including the Master, whose name you could not give us. But you were not one of them, were you? A full list of crew members exists, both survivors and the dead. There was never a signalman named Flack, indeed there was no-one of that name on board.

The glass moved speedily away from the centre. To nobody's surprise, it headed for the letter F.

Mr Flack you were never on that ship. Who were you? You were a Liverpool docker and you heard the story, did you not, how the U-boat crew wept when they heard they had torpedoed children…?

Completing the four-letter word, the glass raced to the letters: IWASTHEREIDIDBLOODYDROWN

It paused briefly then: IDROWNEDLIKEYOULLDROWNIKNOW-ITYOULLDROWNTOO

The transcript was messy, jittery, arrowed and scribbled, but it showed Alan pressing on: *Why are you lying, Flack? Where are you? Are you in hell? Is Satan there? Is the devil with you?*

The glass was now zooming back and forth repeatedly to the same letters as we sought vainly to keep track and Maureen scribbled frantically: DROWNDROWNALLDROWNALLFUCKINGDROWN

I just remembered thinking, this glass is getting hot, my finger feels it. Again and again it spelled out the same furious cry: YOULLALLD-ROWNYOULLALLDROWNYOULLALLDROWN

Suddenly, Maureen screamed. Alan ducked. I froze and so did Maurice. The glass hurtled from our fingertips out of the ring of letters, flew from the desktop, narrowly missed Alan's head and shattered against the wall. Maurice swore later that the glass fragments quivered on the floor, as if in rage.

The shock of the violence was intense. My heart pounded. Maureen wept softly and Maurice put an arm round her shoulders. Alan's voice was brittle as he tried to joke. 'Well at least we know how we'll all die.' Maureen whispered something and Maurice said, 'No, no, no, not you, pet, you were outside the circle, it's us he means, the dabblers.' I gathered up the paper alphabet and crushed it into a ball, then swept up the glass shards – they were just bits of a broken tumbler again – and thrust the lot into the caretaker's rubbish wagon. I must have picked up Maureen's transcripts, too, and taken them home. I have no memory of it.

Did we discuss the events of the night later? Surely we must, there had to be a post-mortem, some agreed justification for our foolishness. But I remember none. Alan had clearly wanted to show up Seaman Flack as a fraud. But what did that demonstrate? That the spirits were liars, deceivers, bores, blow-hards and show-offs? Just like us? Hardly worth three nights of growing tension, fear and violence. Or was the whole thing a fraud, elaborately engineered by one of us? That was the one scenario none of us accepted.

* * * * *

Smoothing out the transcript now, I wondered just how I was supposed to fit this bizarre episode from my early life into *Fifty Years Before the Masthead?* We had caught some long-dead nobody in a pack of lies and he tried to frighten us with prophecies of our deaths. Already, it was clear, time had proved him wrong. Three of the gang were gone and though certainly Alan drowned, Maurice did not and neither did Frank, as for me, I had come safely through years of amateur sailing which I fully intended to continue.

Vaguely, I wondered if the shock of that night had affected Maurice's health. He was never the most robust person and if I remembered aright, he had not enjoyed a long retirement. On impulse, I went to my laptop and quickly found obituaries in the national trade press. But sub-editors are the grey unknowns of media land, no headlines for them like the celebrity editors and the star writers. So the obits were respectful, sympathetic and short. Maurice Schofield had retired in 1965 after a lifetime with the same group of regional newspapers, rising from junior reporter to chief sub-editor on the group's flagship daily; in March 1967 he had suffered a stroke which rendered him partly disabled; in March 1969, a second stroke took his life.

I searched for the *Echo's* own obituary. It was longer, more fulsome, with a formal photo of Maurice wearing a rare smile above his gingery moustache. But the accounts of his death were equally sketchy: discovered by his wife after the second stroke, rushed to hospital, dead on arrival. Was it a reporter's instinct that left me dissatisfied? There must have been an inquest, I thought. Googling further, I discovered a website, *Coroners' Reports, Northeast England, 1969,* which offered links to individual inquests. It took me only seconds to find *Maurice Hays Wood Schofield, May 21, 1969.* Swiftly I scrolled through the jargon-heavy report. Then I came to the following and froze: 'It is assumed the stroke took place whilst Mr Schofield was standing in his bath taking a shower and that he struck his head on the edge of the bath when he collapsed. He was found by his wife semi-submerged in bath water and swiftly removed to hospital, where he was pronounced dead.' How long he had lain half under water was not stated but a post-mortem showed that there was a considerable quantity of water in his lungs. The overwhelming probability, the Coroner concluded, was that of three elements involved in his demise – the stroke, the blow to his head, the ingestion of bathwater – the third was the overriding causative factor, justifying a verdict of Accidental Death. No matter how often I read it, the meaning was clear: Maurice died in his own bathwater; he drowned, just like Seaman Flack said he would.

It was clear now that both Alan and Maurice drowned, but statistically that was not impossible, and then there was Frank – no water in his demise. I remembered his letters to me … noticing red in his urine, ignoring it, finally going for tests and then getting the verdict, advanced kidney cancer. Then Daphne's infrequent messages about his treatment, his lack of progress, a last wobbly letter from Frank himself enclosing some photos from *Echo* days, and finally from the widow a death announcement and the funeral details, with a heavy hint that I should not bother travelling all the way to Cornwall.

Why suddenly did I feel so deeply saddened? I had long known of his death and we had not seen each other or spoken in years. Perhaps because he was the last link to a better time, with his cackling laugh and his quick wit. They were good times. Seeking other names from the past, I picked up Maureen's transcripts and scanned them for clues, unconnected persons perhaps dropping by as witnesses to our sessions. It was then the fear struck, real fear, deep and paralysing. Maureen had headed Session III in the same way as she did the others, by noting the participants: *Present at Session III: Mr Schofield, Alan, Jerry.* Just the three of us, Maurice, Alan and me, no Frank, he had missed the last night! The fact that Frank died of cancer was irrelevant. He was out of it anyway. He was never cursed. When Flack screamed, 'You will all drown,' he meant Alan, Maurice and me.

I don't know how long I sat, immobile in my luxury stateroom, pondering the implication of our past inquisitiveness. It was only when the *Astoria's* massive engines began to throb seven decks below my feet that I came out of my reverie. It had been Marjorie's idea to book a cruise on a luxury liner. Go round the world, she said, don't stint, get yourself a penthouse, check your research, you have email, telephones. Don't bother calling home, write your memoirs, the world will welcome them. Good, sensible, down-to-earth, ever-protective Marjorie. Trouble was, she could not protect me now.

The sudden dip and yaw of movement, detectable even on a 90,000-ton floating monster like the *Astoria*, reminded me that there had been a weather warning earlier that day. And now I noticed that metal shutters had been lowered over the portholes. The Super-Class butler had been reassuring. We were a day out of Hong Kong in the East China Sea, he said, heading into the Pacific and towards the east coast of Japan. There were numerous modern harbours we could run for if the weather turned really nasty. Wasn't Japan prone to earthquakes and did not earthquakes cause tsunamis? I asked, only half-joking. The butler laughed.

'I think tsunamis are the last thing we need to worry about, Sir Jeremiah. Will you be dressing for dinner or do you want to take something in your suite?'

'Later,' I said, 'I might have something later.'

Now I sit before my laptop, fingers poised above the keyboard. Finally I click and click again and download a current-to-the-minute weather situation map for the East China Sea. Observing the furiously gathering storm that lies in our path, I can only conclude that my long-appointed watery reunion with Alan, Maurice and Frank (and doubtless Seaman Flack, too) will not be long delayed.

The Christmas Party

BALLOONS, coloured, various.
CRACKERS, two-person pulling type.
HATS, gold, crown-shaped, paper.
PUFFERS (noise-makers), limited.

That should do it, I thought, and drew a line on my pad.

I had arranged for the food (sandwiches, angel cakes, custard and jelly, trifle), a gramophone for Musical Chairs to be manned by Mrs White, who would also play the piano for the sing-song, and I had my own shadow-play figures and magical tricks prepared. Also I had my prisoner stories, too, if they wanted.

Only 14 children. There were more when Madge organised things. I had no idea what she planned when she called a meeting that time in the Ivy Lounge. Here we were, she said, all grannies and granddads, our working days long over, receiving the best of care and attention with funny hats and a Christmas tree and the Queen's Speech on telly. But wouldn't it be marvellous, she said, if WE organised something, instead?

That's how the annual children's party started. Naturally, everybody at the Pilgrim's Rest (those who were capable, that is) thought it was a great idea – instead of us sitting around the walls in our armchairs nodding and smiling as the little ones handed over their drawings and their wobbly, home-made gifts, WE would give a party for THEM. That was Madge! Ever the organiser, no problem without a solution.

Madge was a schoolteacher all those years, so she knew what kids liked. The games, traditional ones like Sardines and Hide and Seek and Musical Chairs and Blind Man's Buff and Pinning the Tail on the Donkey, but if they wanted their own new ones, Madge quickly got the hang of them. Before the tea there were the songs, *Underneath The Spreading Chestnut Tree* and *Hands, Knees and Bumps-a-Daisy* and ones from the war they had never heard like *The Quartermaster's Store* ('*There'll be butter, butter rolling down the gutter in the Quartermaster's Store.*') How strange the words must have seemed to them, they didn't understand that butter to us was like fairy food to them. I was elsewhere, of course, wasn't I? For The Duration, as the saying goes. Not that we didn't crave butter, too! That was long before Mrs White and it was Madge who led the sing-song on the old Joanna. She said she was just a keyboard-banger, but I knew better. On quiet afternoons when everyone was nodding off she would play a little piece called, I think *Eliza*, a girl's name anyway, a foreign girl; it was a love song, Madge said, by the composer to his beloved.

I didn't have much to do at the parties, just set out the tables and chairs and stand discreetly ready with a cloth and a bucket, because sure as eggs is eggs, one of the little ones would get over-excited and deposit his custard and jelly over his shoes. I did suggest to Madge one year I should be Santa Claus but she said no, the older boys and girls would not be convinced. Also I think she expected I would muck it up in some way, and she was probably right. But she gave me the job of standing by the door at the end and making sure every boy and girl got a present to take home. And there would be 30 or 40 at the party in those days.

The management never interfered when Madge was in charge, they knew how competent she was. Different now that Madge is gone. There's talk of bouncy castles and face paintings and computer games and the like, all a bit beyond me, and the kids are probably disappointed by my old-fashioned agenda. Matron says she is just my first lieutenant, like I was Madge's, but I know she is keeping a weather eye open, probably after that incident with the fire extinguisher or in case I forget something and I have to admit sometimes I do. That's why I write everything down now. Getting older you get forgetful, so I make sure everything goes down on paper. Like my Christmas party list, which I check yet again. Christmas Eve tomorrow, party at 3 pm, as always. It's very grey outside, "leaden skies" as the weather girl says. Looks like more snow. The children will like that. They get excited by the snow.

* * * * *

It's early and I decide to nip out through the side door, I don't want any fuss about "Where are you going, Mr Cameron?" or "George, you've forgotten your hat", or "Sir, come back, you haven't had your breakfast". So quietly does it, out we go. And my gosh, I was right, it *has* snowed and with a vengeance! Must be a foot and a half, must have snowed all night. And the cold catches your throat, just like at Barth. Funny how Barth comes back to me in the winter. I looked it up once, officially situated in Western Pomerania. I liked the word, Pomerania, like a children's word, a Christmas party fun word, pom-pom-pomerania! But two and a half years behind the wire there and Pomerania wasn't funny, wore out its welcome, you might say.

To say I was surprised to get Madge's call in the middle of the night would be an understatement. I cannot remember when we last talked, but she was quite adamant, we were to meet in Alnwick because she had something to tell me. She wouldn't say what it was but, knowing Madge, it will be important, probably something to do with the Christmas Party this afternoon, maybe something I forgot to do. I always think I have everything squared away, after all the squadron leader made me kind of quartermaster in the POW years because I was so methodical. But methodical is as methodical does, as Madge would say, and if she wants to see me, I will have to make the effort.

Still dark but there are pinpricks of light in the distance and I can hear the Metro rumbling, so that's OK. It will take me into town and I'll catch a bus going north. I've got my pass, I checked. I think there's a rule that pensioners must not use them before nine o' clock or 9.30 but they wouldn't do anything to a pensioner who forgot about that rule, would they? People are good that way.

Feet a bit cold. I should have noticed the snow from my bedroom window and put on my Russian boots as I call them. These shoes are brogues, so they're stout enough but not made for deep snow. But I stamp my feet a lot, that's the classic way to keep the blood circulating. Forgot my gloves, too, dammit, but I can always use the old Pomerania trick and discreetly slip my hand around my … you know… warmest part of the human body they used to say. Anyway, just down the road to the Metro station, and, one thing I have to say in their favour, the coaches are always nice and warm. Just better not fall asleep again, like I did that time when I went all the way to the coast, out for the count.

No harm done, of course, but you do feel a bit stupid, the loss of control I mean. All down to not sleeping properly. Night after night, first two hours fine, then up and down, toss and turn the rest of the night. You end up more exhausted than when you went to bed!

Why are we meeting in Alnwick, you might wonder? It's a pretty town, complete with castle and gardens, a popular spot, always was, but not many will be visiting in December. No puzzle to me, of course. That's where Madge comes from: Marjorie O'Brien, 5ft 5ins, chestnut hair, sparkly brown eyes. She was doing teaching practice but it was the holidays and she was helping out her aunty in the Castle Tearooms. Tea and toasted tea-cakes, tea and scones, tea and cucumber sandwiches cut into triangles, out they would come from the kitchen in an endless stream. Madge was the quickest of the waitresses, so nimble and neat in her black waitress dress and white apron and that tiny hat all the girls had to wear.

I'm not sure about love at first sight, but I couldn't take my eyes off her and being Madge (not that I even knew her name then) she was quick to notice me. I was from Alnmouth, just down the road, not happy about my library job and already making inquiries about military service. Why not, I thought? The things we were hearing about Germany I reckoned I'd be in soon enough whether I liked it or not. Madge was not keen, thought I should wait, but as it turned out she was the one who did the waiting… more than four years before I got back to Alnwick. She knew I'd been shot down and captured and she swore she would wait and so she did. My heart pumped and pumped when we met up again. 'Madge' was all I could say. 'You're a skeleton!' she said. 'We'll have to feed you up.' That was Madge. You could never accuse her of being sentimental.

Only a mile to the station and it's a long mile today. But the Metro carriage when I get there is warm all right, even this early. Not like the first buses in the old days, fresh out of their depot where they've been standing all night, icy cold, you could see your breath. The Metro heat seems to come from under the seat. I ease my shoes off and feel my socks. They're damp. I hold my feet towards the heat source. And I slip my hands under my shirt. I gasp as they touch my skin. The fingers begin to ache. But that's good, means the blood is returning. Only one other passenger in this carriage, a young man, maybe a student, a foreigner I think, looking glumly out at the snow-covered fields.

I need to do some calculating. Getting to Alnwick is quite a trek, then meet with Madge and then back to the Pilgrim's Rest in time for the party at 3 pm. It's going to be tight but there's plenty of public transport on Christmas Eve. It's Christmas Day when everything closes down.

* * * * *

It was the warmth that sent me off, of course, as well as the usual sleep needs. I swore it wouldn't happen but when I woke I was six stops past Central, where I have to get off and catch the Alnwick bus. Easy enough to get out and cross over to the opposite platform, though steps and stairs make my legs go a bit wobbly these days, then catch the train back down the line. But a lot of time is lost. The feet are warm again but I suspect the brogues may be leaking and I can't find the energy to inspect the soles. I run my fingers over them and I can't feel much, but maybe that's my fingers getting cold again. Anyway, I have to watch the station signs and make sure I don't overshoot again. Dammit, so humiliating.

There's a lady sitting opposite, another foreigner, I think, she's nut brown, and she keeps gesturing at me, pointing at my throat. Why doesn't she just say what's wrong, I wonder irritably. Suddenly I realise what's bothering her, my shirt neck is wide open. I'm sure I put a tie on when I got up. I always do, it's generational, we're punctilious about neckties, but there isn't one. I smile at the lady and try to fasten my shirt buttons, the two top ones are open, but my fingers won't work. She watches shyly, then she comes over and brushes my fingers away and fastens the buttons. Then she holds my fingers inside her warm brown hands. I am embarrassed but I don't think she is. I can smell her perfume and feel her softness. Still she says nothing. It's Central and I pull my hands away and get up to leave. In one quick gesture, the way women can do these things, she plucks the scarf from round her neck, a light wool fabric, patterned, Indian figures I think, warm from her body, and winds it deftly round my neck. She then gives me a slight push on my way. I turn back as the train leaves and she is standing at the door. She raises her hand and smiles. She has never said a word. I am crying but I don't know why.

The terminal is busy. City buses come and go and a London bus is filling up with passengers as their luggage is stowed into the side of the vehicle. Country buses are going north and south and I find the stand I need: Morpeth-Alnmouth-Alnwick-Berwick. I'm feeling a bit dizzy but thankfully there are seats for those queuing. Ten minutes to wait. The bus terminal is warm, they have those glowing red heaters suspended above your head, but it is bad outside. Great swirls of snow are battering against the glass walls. This will surely slow down travel times, I think, which is a bit worrying because there is something I have to get back for this afternoon. For the moment I can't remember what, then it comes – of course, the kids' Christmas party, *my* party in a sense, can't miss that.

I ask the driver how much to Alnmouth and he says, aren't you a "senior," meaning pensioner? Of course, I say, and show him my pass. Then you travel free, granddad, did you forget? He's a nice man, he smiles and says, "Welcome aboard." I ask how long to Alnmouth and he tells me but says it might be longer on account of the snow. I've forgotten how long he said. I know he'll do his best, he looks like a conscientious man. The bus is a double decker but I take a seat on the lower deck. It's quite warm, so I might doze again, but I know the driver will make sure I get off at my destination. The drivers on these country buses are much nicer than on the short city routes.

The snow drives past the window as we move into the countryside. There's a pine forest and a large church and a glimpse of the sea. It reminds me of somewhere… Barth, is it? Stalag Luft I? There was a forest and a church and the sea there. Of course, I am not there, am I? It seems so real but it's just a memory, something in my mind. I'm on a bus in the north of England, going to meet my wife in Alnmouth. And I have something else to do today, in the afternoon. It will come to me.

* * * * *

'Come on, old timer, Alnmouth, time to go.' It's the driver. He comes back and helps me up. Did I have a bag? No. A case? No. Where's your hat? He finds it on the rack and puts it on my head and guides me off the bus. 'Mind how you go, granddad.'

I begin to walk out of town. Madge called me last night, that's certain, but I think I made another mistake. I got off at Alnmouth and Madge lives in Alnwick. That is to say, she did. We did. But that was years ago, before we went into the home. This is confusing.

There's a whole lot of buildings out there across the fields – four prison compounds and the German building in the centre, "the Oasis" we call it, full of flowers and shrubs. And there's the wire, miles and miles of it, two rows four feet apart attached to 10-ft posts. Can't see from here but there'll be a Guard Tower further on, plenty of them.

There's something sticking out of my left sleeve. It's like a block of wood and I have been trying to shake it off but it just stays there. I rap it with my right hand. I lift it up and it looks familiar. It drops down and I feel it hit my side. The snow is coming down hard again and it's difficult to see the camp, but I don't mind, I don't feel cold any more. I think I had a scarf, it came from India, but now it's gone. My hat, too. Where did that go? The strange thing is I am *outside* the wire. They don't allow that, I could be shot if they see me. Where are the other guys? My mate, Nick Alkemade, the famous rear gunner who survived a fall of 18,000 feet without a parachute? Well, that's what everybody said. And that guy Donald Whatsit who became a film star, and all those thousands of Yanks?

Oops, the wire! Walked right into it, watch where you're going, Flight Sergeant! No guard towers, that's strange, but there should be a gate, somewhere along here. If I keep walking I'm bound to find it. Funny, how I don't feel cold any more and the snow is blasting right into my face! What I feel is tired. More than tired, sleepy. I think I'll stretch out here for a while, these old bones have had enough for one day. I have something important to do later, but for the life of me I can't remember what it is. Funny how snow makes you warm. It should make you cold, shouldn't it? But down here it's so cosy. Time for a little sleep, meet Madge later.

A Change of Shifts

'PADDY,' HIS MOTHER WHISPERED, 'PADDY.' SHE KNOCKED SOFTLY on the bedroom door. In the 5 am darkness, the bed creaked. 'It's Joe,' she said, 'he's poorly.' She hesitated. 'Can you turn in for him?'

'Oh God!' Paddy's low groan was muffled by the pillow. 'What's wrong with him?'

'He just says he feels bad. The thing is, you know, losing his shift money, what with Dad and all…'

'Why did he send you? Why didn't he ask me himself…?' The ticking of the alarm clock was the only sound in the room. '... because he knows the answer he would bloody get.'

'Paddy, he's just a lad…'

The elder brother broke in. 'What's he on?'

'Six till two. You've got plenty time to get up to the Betsy. And I've got to get over to let the night cleaners away.'

She hovered at the half-open door.

'Bloody Joe,' said Paddy, swinging his legs out of the bed. He gasped as the icy bedroom air hit him.

'Thanks, son, you've got a good heart. Try and have a word with your brother before you go. Don't forget to take his bait tin, it's on the table.'

Downstairs, Paddy half-filled a kettle in the kitchen and fired the gas under it, then lit a Woodbine from the gas flame and coughed deeply. 'Bloody Joe,' he muttered, 'bloody brother Joe!' He poured the hot water into the pots-washing basin and swiftly sluiced his face, neck and chest. Back in his bedroom with a mug of milky tea, he slipped into his work clothes and pulled on his pit boots, activities which sent a faint miasma of coal dust into the chill air.

On the kitchen table sat a school tin decorated with pictures of Donald Duck and Mickey Mouse and marked "Joe Brady" and Paddy lifted the lid. His mother had already replaced Joe's cocoa with twists of tea leaves and sugar which Paddy preferred. He slipped the box into his overcoat pocket.

Joe slept in the nook under the stairs and Paddy knocked on the wood above his head and slid the curtain aside. 'Hoo, wor kid,' he said. 'What's up?'

'Sorry, Paddy,' Joe said, croakily, 'just feeling bad.' He hesitated. 'You know, shaky.'

Paddy peered into the dark space. 'Too much reading, that's your bloody problem. Give the books a rest, man.'

He rattled the curtain back into place and walked to the front door. Passing the front room, where his father now slept, he rapped on the door with his knuckles and called 'Da, tara.' There was a burst of coughing and Paddy went out and pulled the front door behind him.

* * * * *

Ten minutes went by, then checking the pocket watch on the floor by his cot, Joe poked his bare feet into leather slippers and pulled a hairy brown dressing gown around his shoulders. These were two items of clothing whose purchase Paddy had observed without comment, though Joe did not need the gift of clairvoyance to deduce his thoughts. Silence spoke volumes in the Brady household.

From a battered suitcase under his bed, Joe produced a white shirt and a tie and from the wardrobe in Paddy's room he lifted down his brother's navy suit. Joe was a year younger but they were identical in physique and the shirt, suit and tie instantly made him the best-dressed young man in Scotswood.

He lit a cigarette and checked his pockets – handkerchief, change, wallet. From the wallet, he plucked a letter, which he smoothed out and read, checking the address and the appointment – 10 am – for the umpteenth time.

He shrugged on his own dark overcoat but not his cap. Instead he took his father's grey trilby from the rack behind the front door. It fitted perfectly. Joe raised his hand to knock on the door of the front room, but changed his mind and walked quietly out of the house.

Turning down a cinder path flanked by straggly weeds and dandelions made grubby with coal smoke, he walked to the tram stop and checked his watch again. Ten minutes for the next one into the city.

* * * * *

The Betsy pit's hooters sounded at 1.30, but this was not a shift-change for they went on and on, drilling a message of alarm over the rows of white-washed colliery cottages, past the slag heap and down to the city road.

Joe, in the act of returning Paddy's suit to the wardrobe, stiffened. All three of the Betsy's sirens had been activated, he realised, a full-scale emergency calling fire, ambulance and rescue teams. 'Please God, no,' he whispered, 'Paddy, no, no!'

Throwing on his work clothes, Joe raced past the pit cottages, dodged between the slag-filled tubs clanking automatically up and down the wagon way, and on up to the pit head.

The yard was filling rapidly with women, many still wearing aprons, hair awry, others with coats flung over their heads or shawls pulled tight like bonnets. Off-duty miners running into the yard were being marshalled into rescue teams by deputies whom Joe recognised but knew better than to approach. A red fire truck drove in, bell clanging.

Joe saw that the winding gear high over the pit head was stopped, but that might simply mean the cages were emptying or loading. There was no smoke, no signs of fire and he had heard no explosions, though respirators and masks were being distributed to the rescue teams.

Feeling a hand on his shoulder, Joe turned: Bob Etherington, a neighbour and a two-to-ten Betsy man. 'Joe, you're here! What happened?' Etherington's face was a mixture of relief and surprise. 'How did you get out?'

'I was never down,' Joe said. 'Paddy took the shift for me. I was poorly. What's happened?'

'Poor Paddy,' said Etherington, not answering. Then seeing Joe's stricken face, he said quickly. 'It might be all right. They say it's old water and maybe gas. The Betsy's a wet pit, we all know that, but some men are supposed to be safe, the cages are bringing them up. Some others are finding old walk-outs or ventilation shafts. Joe Robson is down there. He knows the layout.'

Involuntarily, they glanced up at the colliery wheels.

'There, look,' shouted Bob. One was starting to turn. 'They're coming up,' he exclaimed, pointing excitedly.

Joe scanned the growing crowd of women and spotted his mother, still in the green uniform of a Betsy cleaner, features anguished and working. They hugged briefly and he told her what little he knew. 'But Joe,' she said, remembering, 'you're not well, you should be in bed. Why did...'

She was interrupted by a cry, 'Joe?' Elaine, ten yards away, stood stock still, staring at him, incredulous, joyous. Joe approached slowly, hand outstretched. 'Elaine.'

'But you're in-bye, Joe, you're six till two this week, you told me.'

Joe explained about the change but still she stared.

'No, Joe, I saw Paddy this morning, early, at the tram stop going into town. Just from the back but it was Paddy, I'm sure, he had his navy suit on.'

Joe's mother's puzzlement turned to anger. 'Elaine! Be pleased you have your boyfriend. I have a son who might be dying down there this minute.'

Elaine turned away, weeping softly. And there the three remained through the long dark afternoon and evening, as team after team of masked rescuers went down and groups of men and boys emerged, some coughing or half-drowned, most naked to the waist, their skinny white torsos shining in the growing gloom. At first the survivors came up in small groups, instantly smothered by joyous relatives, then in twos or threes, then singly after long gaps. Paddy was never among them.

* * * * *

The first great funeral was held nearly two months later when 23 of the 38 men and boys lost in the March 30 Betsy disaster were buried in Elswick cemetery. Ornate, glass-sided funeral carriages, each drawn by two black horses and carrying a single coffin, formed a procession three miles long. Among the three-deep crowds watching in pouring rain were many of the 110 miners who survived because they were far enough from the burst to reach safety in time.

Sitting in St Margaret's Church for the funeral service, Joe reflected that Bob Etherington had been right. It was water and gas. Two charges had been fired to bring down a jud of coal and at first all seemed well. But beyond the coal slab were the abandoned workings of the neighbouring Paradise pit, widely known to be dangerously flooded. When Joe Robson spotted water spurting from the two shot holes, he shouted, 'Run lads, out, get out, for Christ's sake.' But the jud collapsed and a putrid torrent roared into the Betsy, propelling poisonous swathes of choking black damp ahead of it. Most of the victims were working close to the breakout and were gassed or drowned within minutes. The fury and speed of the onslaught gave them no chance of escape.

St Margaret's was filled by close kin of the 23 while their coffins remained in the carriages outside. Joe sat between Elaine, tense and weepy, and his mother, bowed by grief for Paddy and strained by money fears. Medication and doctors' bills were mounting for her sick husband and she worried how long Dr Coxon's forbearance would last. The Betsy was now closed for investigation and looked like remaining shut for many months, perhaps for ever. She had lost her cleaning job, there was no compensation for dead Paddy and no work for Joe.

It was the recovery of her son's body on the seventh day which had seemed to bring his mother a sense of closure. It was then that she raised Elaine's questions about the man in the navy suit. Quickly, succinctly Joe explained. She took his hand and for the first time, wept. But whether she wept for the death of her oldest son or the survival of her youngest, or in misery over the deception Joe did not know.

As the vicar's prayers droned on, remote and not registering, Joe reached into his pocket for the letter he had received that morning. In embossed type it was headed "Workers' Educational Association." He spread the single sheet with his forefinger and glanced over the visible fragments of sentences which already he knew by heart: "... your interview on March 30... happy to offer... tutorial class... sustained studies over three years... higher academic level..."

He recalled Paddy's last words to him, "Give the books a rest, man," and he smiled slightly. Then, unnoticed by his mother and Elaine, he tore the letter into fragments, and seeing no waste bin, he dropped the pieces into a collection plate by the church door marked "Disaster."

As they walked into the rainy midday, Elaine took his arm and whispered, 'I heard they're opening a new seam at High Pit, Joe. You could try there, they will be taking on.'

Joe nodded.

'It's a job, after all, isn't it, Joe?'

Joe did not reply. He took his mother's arm and all three followed Paddy's coffin to its burial place.

Little Wolfie

Grunting softly, Doctor Spiegelman lowered his bulk into the bedside chair and took his patient's hand. 'So it's all over, Klara, no complications, no catastrophes, just as I said.'

The dark-haired woman smiled weepily.

'And like the announcements always say, Both well!' He squeezed her bony fingers. 'So are we going to get a peek at this little devil who has caused us all so much trouble?'

She pulled back the lacy coverlet. He was curled sideways, a thin face, thatch of dark hair, a bubble of saliva on the lips. The baby squirmed as the warm blanket was removed and squinted hard in the doctor's direction. The slits of eyes were cobalt blue.

'Dark brown hair and bright blue eyes,' said the doctor, smiling, 'that will bring the girls running.'

The tiny features twisted unhappily in the unaccustomed cold and Klara pulled the blanket back, tucking it in all round. Then she kissed the baby's forehead. 'My little Wolfie,' she whispered, 'my precious Wolf.'

She glanced shyly, abashed, at her physician. 'You were right all along, of course, it was the right thing to do, but Doctor Spiegelman, I was so frightened, it didn't feel like the others, not right somehow, and Alois was so against. I was full of fear.'

'Klara, my dear, I have cared for your family for years. I saw you through your childhood ailments, watched you grow up, attended your other confinements. I knew what you were thinking and I knew it was wrong. If I pressed you beyond the boundaries of the medical relationship, well, forgive me. I'm just a simple GP, but we old family doctors, we know about these things. And it all turned out for best in the end, didn't it?'

It had and Klara was grateful, but Doctor Spiegelman had no idea of the agonies she had gone through In the months since she told Alois she was pregnant again.

* * * * *

Perhaps it was the previous deaths that made this time so different. She had always been overjoyed when she felt the first changes in her body, the certainty of a new fruitfulness long before the doctor's confirmation. But losing two toddlers and a helpless infant to diphtheria in a single dreadful winter two years ago robbed her of joyful anticipation and filled her with dread.

Worse, her body was seized with pains, sporadic, unexpected, almost unnatural, as if the new life inside her was seizing control, demanding power over her fragile frame. Morning sickness was remorseless, and though she tried to hide the spasms in her womb that came as she sat by the fire at night, they were enough to send Alois storming angrily from the room.

For weeks the husband said nothing – his own dalliances set constraints upon his tongue – but then he began bringing newspapers from the office with selected advertising notices underlined in red. It was not difficult to deduce what was meant by "irregularity," "obstruction" and "menstrual suppression," all problems which the advertisers claimed could be solved by ingestion of *Lesser's Woman's Friends, Angela's Vegetable Compound* or *Madame Drunette's Lunar Pills for all female complaints.*

One advertisement, for *Dr Dieter's French Renovating Pills*, declared boldly: "Pregnant women, do not use! They produce a miscarriage."

Klara pushed the prints aside with little more than a glance, infuriating her husband. 'Look at them, read them,' Alois shouted, shaking the paper so it tore. 'Look, at the bottom there, ladies who will help, experienced midwives, see their addresses.'

Klara knew exactly what these ladies offered. Young women learned all these things long before marriage, things their husbands never knew. Mothers, grandmothers, the local midwife – every street seemed to have one – even maiden aunts were more than ready with the clinical details: injected solutions to flush out the uterus, sitting over a pot of steam, hot baths, vacuum devices, Spanish fly, candles, hair-curling irons, knitting needles. And so the hated irregularity, the unwanted obstruction would be no more, consigned to the privy, out of sight and forever out of mind.

Alois had offered to pay for treatment from his government salary, for pills or anything more, and Klara wondered at the fierceness of his opposition. True, he was not the ideal warm and playful father but he had always accepted the normality of big families – indeed she was sure he had children she knew nothing about. But now it seemed that he feared their fourth child in person, that somehow, if brought to term and reared, it might somehow destroy him.

One day when the pains became unbearable, Klara pulled one of Alois's newspapers from the scuttle on the hearth and printed down the name and address of a midwife "with proven experience in relieving troubled women of their fears."

But first in desperation she called upon Doctor Spiegelman and in the privacy of his inner office poured out her fears. Perturbed, he examined her closely, grunting, wheezing and muttering. 'You are not far gone, you should not be having such pain,' he said. 'And everything is perfectly normal, baby lying right, the correct size.' He pondered. Klara was not hysterical – indeed the Polzi family tended to be stoics – but her distress was genuine and he was disturbed by her remark that she 'would do anything to end it.'

'Klara,' he said, softly, 'you have a baby in there, a tiny defenceless gramme or two of life. He, or maybe she, depends on you for life. He has to grow, this hurts your body but it is the cycle of life. If he is not allowed to grow to term he will die, this speck of life.'

Klara raised a tear-stained face. 'I know, Doctor, but the pain…'

He interrupted. 'And your Church. I am not of your faith, but your pastors, on such an issue, they offer no room to negotiate, no soft words. What you are thinking is not permitted. Life is life.'

* * * * *

Alois was furious. 'You went to that fat Jew doctor,' he raged, 'and you listened to him! Klara, is he the one suffering from pains? Is he sharing our bed at night as you cry and kick and jerk with spasms? Did he not see your black, pouchy eyes and your stringy hair? Did he not ask about your weight? About that constant, endless vomiting caused by this thing inside you?'

Klara tried to be calm. 'He acknowledged that I had lost weight. He said it was not unusual for a pregnant mother on her third or fourth child to meet with unexpected problems, a rough passage, he said. He knows my family. It won't go wrong, he says. I should see it through.'

'A rough passage!' For the first time in their marriage, Alois struck out at his wife. His flying stein hit her below the breasts and the beer splashed into her face.

'Tomorrow we are going into Braunau,' he said, 'and we are going to end it.'

Klara, sobbing, wondered if the stein had been thrown at her face or at her womb.

* * * * *

The address in the advertisement took them to a row of low cottages between the public baths and St Stephen's Church with its soaring spire overlooking the River Inn. At number three, Madame Fleischer, resolver of ladies' problems, cautiously opened the green door. To Klara, a nod and 'Please step inside.' Then dismissively to Alois, 'Thank you, sir, goodbye.'

The woman's hands were clean, Klara noted gratefully as the examination began. In a corner behind the bent back, half-concealed under a white cloth, metal instruments glinted. A rubber suction cup lay in full sight.

'Everything is fine with you,' Madame Fleischer finally declared, straightening up. 'Not too far along. There should be no problems. There is another lady first, so if you can return to the waiting room and just relax. Please do not worry, I have done thousands of these procedures.' She paused. 'And about the fee? The gentleman...?'

'I have it,' Klara said, tapping her breast, and the abortionist nodded, smiling for the first time.

The waiting room was the cottage hallway with the boot cupboard removed. The operating room was the sitting/dining room beyond the inside door. Klara settled into an armchair but relaxation was out of the question. She could hear grunts from behind the door and these quickly became wails which set Klara's nerves on edge.

At one point, Madame Fleischer popped her head around the door. She looked harassed. 'Please don't worry,' she said. 'This is all quite normal. Try to relax again, Madame, blot it out. I'll come to you soon.'

But relaxing was not an option. Restlessly turning about in her chair, seeking ease, she glanced out of the window and her eyes fell on a metal garbage bin behind the cottage. There were red streaks down the silver, corrugated outside. The lid was insecurely slanted over the bulging contents and a brown paper parcel poked above the rim. It was this that was leaking the glutinous rivulets of blood.

Rising abruptly, Klara reached a trembling hand into her frock and dropped Alois's money-stuffed envelope onto her chair. She ran from the cottage, stumbling, leaving the green door banging behind her.

* * * * *

'Alois can't have been pleased,' Doctor Spiegelman remarked, absently stroking the baby's dimpled knuckles with his forefinger.

'I was surprised,' said Klara. 'It was as if he expected nothing would come of it. He seemed angrier that I left the money, though I knew he wouldn't pursue it. He would not want his workmates to know.'

'And the pains?'

'That was a help, too. They started to ease and we could sleep at last. As you know yourself, the last months were fine. It was strange. I don't know why.'

'Don't you?' said the doctor smiling wryly. 'It was your son! He knew he was safe.'

'Oh doctor, really!'

'Klara, he knew he would live, he would survive to become something great, a leader of men, a shaper of national destinies!'

Klara laughed. 'A simple schoolmaster would be fine, or a postal clerk like his father.'

The doctor levered himself up, snapped his instrument bag shut and reached for his hat. 'One thing puzzles me, Klara – you call him Little Wolfie. Why? There are no Wolfgangs in your family. Or in Alois's either, as far as I know.'

Klara shook her head. 'Not Wolfgang, Doctor Spiegelman, Adalwulf – you know, *adal* and *wulf*, Noble Wolf.'

'Ah, neat! Very neat,' said the doctor, nodding. 'But isn't Adalwulf a bit old-fashioned these days, bit hoity-toity?'

'It is old-fashioned, Doctor, but dignified. He will get Adolf anyway, like all the boys do.'

Doctor Spiegelman raised his arm in salute: 'Noble Wolf Adolf, leader of the pack, shaper of destinies, ruler of nations. We hail you. The future is yours.'

Klara smiled sleepily and the doctor said, 'I'll let myself out, I know the way. Keep the little fellow warm. I said everything would be all right, didn't I? And I was right, wasn't I?'

Time to Go

'Good morning, Kimanzi my friend, two G & T's please, plenty ice, also give me a packet of those …' he stopped abruptly. 'What's this, then?' pointing to the barman's bare head. 'Where's your *tarboosh*?'

'Fez gone, Bwana Tony.' Kimanzi grinned. 'New time.'

'The committee approved this?'

'Yes, Bwana, next thing *kanzu*' – he plucked at his long white robe – 'and this,' the scarlet cummerbund.

'Then you'll get a bow tie and tight pants and a bum freezer, I suppose, like those little ponces in London.'

Kimanzi's smile faded.

'Stop it, Tone,' his wife muttered.

'Just banter, darling,' as he picked up the drinks.

'He's only a barman.'

'Well, I mean… fucking New Time!'

He turned back to the bar. 'New Time not yet, Kimanzi, two more months before paradise dawns!'

'Yes, sah,' said the barman tonelessly.

It was an hour before lunch and the club bar was empty but for an elderly man in khaki shorts sitting at a corner table, in front of him a bottle of cold beer and a stained slouch hat.

'Well, look who's here,' exclaimed Tony Aldington's wife. 'Hello Pinky, can we join you?'

'A pleasure, Charley,' said the old man, rising with measured politeness.

They settled on either side of his table in the casual way of old friends. 'So, Pinky, lovely to see you. But what brings you down from that mansion of yours?'

'Sonya,' Pinky said shortly. His daughter was landing from London in a few hours with Nigel, his ten-year-old grandson. 'The boy's only been to Africa once when he was an infant, and she says she wants him to see it "before it changes forever" – her words.' He paused. 'But also, I think she wants to make one last effort, face to face, to winkle me out of here.'

'Is that such a bad idea?' asked Tony. 'You probably heard we're going.'

Pinky looked up. 'The Aldingtons are leaving! My God, Tony, your family has been in the country for yonks!'

'It's the only sensible thing. Don't think it doesn't hurt us, too.'

'South, I suppose?'

'They're still our kind of people there.'

'And when the South goes?'

'We reckon they're good for another forty, fifty years, enough for us. And certainly for you, Pinky. You can't rattle around for ever in that Mingati mausoleum of yours. They're not going to leave you alone, you know. It's fine farmland in the Uplands and a unique house and they want it.'

Pinky looked up. 'They've already been, Tony. That Waiyaki fellow, the new MP, came sniffing around. I reminded him what the Big Man said – he wants our people to stay after independence, to farm, he's a farmer himself, to produce, to feed the people, to take our place in the new nation.'

'Oh, sure,' Tony laughed shortly. 'And what did the creep Waiyaki say?'

'He just asked how many acres, how many tractors, how many workers, how much we pay them? Of course, he knows all that.'

'Of course he does. So what could be clearer? He hasn't got the power now but he will in December. It's time to sell up and go.'

The old man groaned softly. 'And join Sonya and that bore of a husband of hers in Eastbourne where they can 'keep an eye' on me? Oh yes, and one thing I have to be sure about – repatriate the proceeds of the sale before independence dawns!'

He smiled mirthlessly and Tony and Charlotte exchanged glances.

'Come on, Pinky, they're just being sensible. What else will you do? You've had an amazing life in Africa. Nothing lasts for ever.'

* * * * *

Next morning the old man and the boy stood on a rocky outcrop high in the Uplands, staring in silence at the billowing mist and moiling cloud which filled the great valley below their feet. It would be another hour before the equatorial sun would dispel the chill of dawn, dissolving the whiteness and revealing the tracks, streams, beehive huts and vast tracts of bush far below. 'We're above the sky,' Nigel murmured, 'it's magic.' Pinky nodded, half-smiling.

'There's a path down the escarpment,' the old man said, 'I'll show you where we hunted, the two of us.'

'Is it where you got all those heads, the ones in your house?'

Sonya had pleaded jet lag the night before and retired early while Pinky showed his grandson around Mingati, a massive, creaking, *makuti*-roofed homestead of indigenous woods, polished and carved, varnished and where necessary reinforced, the first two-storey home in the Uplands. Nigel knew that his grandfather surveyed the ground, designed the house and led a team of local workers in constructing it from the foundations up. 'Whatever else he did or didn't do, that was an amazing feat,' his mother said. But when Nigel asked why he called it Mingati, Sonya did not answer.

Entering the vast sitting room, the boy had gazed around the walls spellbound. The Big Five were there, mounted on polished wood plaques: Lion, Leopard, Elephant, Buffalo and Rhino. And in the hallway, Pinky identified a cheetah, wild pig, hartebeest and impala. Nigel pointed to a head in a corner snarling for eternity through bared fangs.

'That one looks dangerous, Grandad. Look at its teeth,' he said excitedly.

Pinky shook his head.

'That one's a joke, old fellow, killed by an idiot politician from Britain, one of the independence brigade, who fancied himself as a big white hunter. That's a wild dog, son, horrible thing, not worth the wood we put it on. It's there to mock him and his lot.'

Hours later, moving carefully down the escarpment, Nigel decided to risk his grandfather's wrath – his mother had warned he could be testy.

'Grandad, why do they call you Pinky?' he asked. The old man frowned. 'I mean,' hastily, 'if you want to say.' There was a long delay, then the hunter/house-builder held up his right hand.

'How many fingers, boy?'

'Three.'

'And which one is missing?'

'The little one.'

'And what do they call the little one?' Nigel did not know. 'They call it the pinky and I haven't got one so they gave me that nickname.' The irony escaped the boy. The old man said, 'It's a kind of humour.'

'But Grandad …' puzzled, earnest.

'Yes, you want to know *how* did I lose it?'

'Yes, sir, how?'

Pinky rolled up the sleeve of his safari jacket. His naked white forearm was thin as a stick, bone barely covered by skin, dark brown gouges showing where the flesh had been stripped out, never to grow back. 'It was a leopard, son, the cleverest of them all, the one that scares hunters most, and a female, too. She came out of a tree, knocked us over, sent Min's gun flying, then tried to eat my face.' The man's blue eyes darkened as he remembered – the jaws agape, saliva streaming over the teeth, angry eyes, a huge weight crushing him. 'I did the only thing I could, I thrust my arm down her throat.'

'Gosh, Grandad, down her throat,' whispered Nigel. 'But …?'

'But why didn't she bite my arm off? Because my fist was choking her, gagging her. So what did she do, the clever old thing? She just clamped those big yellow fangs together and began to pull back and that's when she scraped my arm to the bone, peeled the flesh right off. At the time I didn't feel it, I just knew I was nearly free, but suddenly she convulsed and the teeth locked down. That's when I lost my pinky and the edge of my hand. But it was over. She had taken a bullet in the brain from my companion.'

They walked on in silence for a while.

'Who was Min, granddad?'

'I told you, he was my companion.'

'But who *was* he?' There was a pause.

'You ask too many questions, boy.' The old man walked ahead as the valley bottom neared.

'Grandad,' the boy said, 'my name is Nigel.' Bird sounds emerged from the bush as the light brightened. Pinky slowed down.

'Nigel,' he said, savouring the sound.

'*Pole, toto, pole sana*. I stand rebuked, Nigel it is.'

* * * * *

Late that night, Nigel woke trying to define the sounds that whirled in his brain. Dreams? Airplane engines? Bush noises? Grandad told him monkeys often fought and squabbled in the trees behind Mingati or on the roof of the house, just family quarrels but violent and noisy. But this wasn't baboons. He knew the sound of his mother's shrill voice. From Pinky's lofty sitting room, he heard her tones, varied in pitch – urgent, arguing, almost pleading. They were counterpointed by rare, low murmurs from Grandad. But the escarpment had drained the boy's young energies and soon he slept again.

In the morning Nigel found the old man standing alone, silhouetted against the picture window giving onto the valley.

'*Jambo, toto*,' Pinky said, 'Legishon's in the kitchen. He'll make breakfast for you, juice, eggs, whatever you want.' Nigel didn't move.

'Does *toto* mean child, Grandad?'

'Child, yes, little one/kid/baby/boy/girl/infant.' He paused, 'And, because I know you are going to ask, *pole sana* means…'

'… "very sorry." '

'Yes,' Pinky turned away from the window, "very sorry." '

There was a moment of silence, then, 'Your mum has driven over to the Aldingtons, they're old friends.'

'Was there a row, Grandad?'

The old man gestured to the boy to sit.

'Your mother wants me to go back to England, leave here, sell Mingati and the farm or what's left of it and go and live in a granny flat in Eastbourne, that's what she called it, a granny flat, attached to the house apparently. She thinks I'm too old for a new country. Trouble is…' his voice slowed, 'she has forgotten what it was like – wild little Sonya, skinny bare brown legs, playing with the kitchen totos, fearless, running free.'

'She had the flat built onto our house for you, Grandad, she painted it herself. You would live with us is the plan. I'd have a new grandad. It would be ace. You could fly back with us, or maybe later after you've sold everything.'

The old man said nothing.

'But you won't, will you, Grandad?'

'Let's see what Legishon can get for you.'

Seated on the verandah, Nigel ate paw-paw and pineapple, eggs and sausages with chapatis and juice and listened to his grandfather.

'Your mother left before the country caught her, do you understand? I mean this' – he gestured at the lifting mist, the acacia trees in the middle distance and far away the emerging, snow-topped mountain peaks. 'Your grandmother whipped her away, back "home" as she said, to England, before the Africa virus took hold. Mingati wasn't built then and living wasn't easy. My wife never took to it. Or to my friends.'

'Was it Min?'

Pinky's mind went back to the sour grimness of Magda's face whenever his African friend's name came up. Min had tried to help, offered to use his African expertise in a million ways. But she wouldn't bend. 'Friend?' she said. 'Too much of a friend! Too friendly a friend!'

Nigel brought his granddad back. 'Was his full name Mingati?'

'Yes, it was.'

'Same as the house.'

'Named for him. It has a meaning, Nigel. African names have meanings. Mingati means, 'One who is fast and does not lag behind.' That was Mingati, fast as the wind and always upfront. It's a lion name. Min had already killed his lion for the tribe.'

The old man's voice broke and for a terrible moment, Nigel thought he was going to cry, but instead he began to talk.

'It started with the war, fifty years ago. I'd been kicking around for a while, fresh from England, climbing, hunting, exploring, did some sailing at the Coast, everything unbelievably cheap, no rules, great weather, empty spaces and such a relief from our depressed old country. A lot came out, public school mostly, knew each other. Then it was 1914 and that changed everything. There was a German East Africa in those days. Did you know that? Disciplined people the Germans, strong rulers, a real threat.'

'So were you a soldier, Grandad?'

'King's African Rifles… Tanga, Taveta, around Kilimanjaro, Neu-Moshi… lots of skirmishes. Mingati was my batman, same age we reckoned, looking for adventure before the tribe called him home. Tall like all his people, well over six feet, handsome, clever.'

'A batman?'

'Kind of officer's personal servant. They often didn't fight, but you couldn't stop Min. He was never more than a pace away from me, guide and protector – and servant, if you must – all in one. When the war ended we stayed together. It wasn't usual, two men, black and white, officer and Other Rank, there were remarks, but we didn't care. I told you "companions." We were friends.'

'Was that when you started hunting?'

'The country was still raw in those days, Nigel, no fences, no game wardens, the wildlife were in charge. We began to be hired by the colonial authorities, the DCs, the PCs, or by individual settlers or groups of farmers to track down predators destroying their crops or attacking cattle, sometimes even the natives. Man-eaters could get a taste for blood, you know, and they would always come back.'

'Did you always get them, the predators?'

'We had to produce the corpse – lion, leopard, whatever. That was the deal: No hides/no pay.'

'Did you hunt elephants, Grandad?'

Pinky paused, reluctant. 'We did, early on, for the ivory, prices were good, but I stopped it.' He shook his head… 'those great, grey creatures shivering when the bullet hit, shrinking, collapsing, their huge hearts failing, down onto their knees, helpless as babies. It wasn't brave.' He followed Nigel's eyes to the elephant head on the wall. 'She was my last, a matriarch. I will destroy her.' The old man fell silent, then, 'Let's go for a walk, son.'

They toured the barns, empty at this time, vast, lofty and cooled with water sprays; the servants' quarters where snotty-nosed *totos* shouted '*Jambo, Mzee*' shrilly in chorus at the sight of Pinky; a garage accommodating two cars – one a saloon and a big-wheeler for rural terrain, four tractors and trailers, a vast baler, a muck-spreader, coils of wire and on the walls spanners grouped in inverted triangles according to size; beyond that the locked petrol store.

Outside, Nigel asked, 'Grandad, there was an old wreck of a motor-bike in a corner.'

'Oh, you saw that? That old wreck is, or was, a 1920, 500cc Rover motor cycle, very popular at its time, light and nimble, easy to handle on our dirt roads. I bought if for your granny.'

'For Grandmother! A motor-bike?'

‘That way she didn’t need to sit in a car with an African.’

‘Oh.’

* * * * *

The war was over and Pinky was in the port buying supplies for a safari into the central forest area. HE the Ambassador happened to be down from the capital so of course there was a garden party.

‘That’s where I first saw Magda,’ Pinky said, ‘sitting straight-backed under a date palm in the Consul’s garden. Women wore round hats in those days with white veils. She lifted the veil when I walked up. I had never seen a more beautiful woman and I swore to myself there and then she would be my wife.’

Nigel smiled.

‘I quickly realised it would not be easy. She was unhappy behind those piercing blue eyes, restless, always peering past you, like looking for a way of escape.’

‘She hated Africa,’ Nigel said. ‘Mum told me once, said she was ‘wounded’ somehow. She wouldn’t explain.’

‘William Charlton, remittance man, handsome and a bounder, but she adored him. They met in London, he brought her out here to marry her, then ditched her. It was a huge scandal. Everybody in the colony knew about it. Desperately humiliating for Magda. I made her my wife and built a house for her, we had a baby, but all she ever wanted was to return to England.’

* * * * *

Dinner that night was not easy. Between Legishon’s soft-footed visits to the table, Sonya announced that during her visit to the Aldingtons she had telephoned BOAC and booked a return flight to London, 9.00 p.m. tomorrow, for herself and Nigel. For a fleeting moment, she looked at her father, who looked away. He said he would drive them to the airport but she said that was all right, Tony Aldington had agreed to pick them up and Charlotte would go along, too, for a bit of company. They would leave here mid-morning, lunch at the club then shop for some Africana bits and pieces for friends back home before the long drive out to the airport.

Pinky asked could they not stay a few more days, he and Nigel had already become good friends, but Sonya said the new school term was starting for the boy and she would have new arrangements to make with regard to the granny flat.

Through all this, Nigel sat stiffly, close to tears.

When Legishon brought coffee, Sonya shook her head, *hapana*, no, she was tired and needed a bath and had all the packing to do. Turning at the foot of the great staircase, she addressed Nigel mock-severely, 'Don't sit round past midnight listening to your grandad's old war stories.' Her son tried to smile.

The grandfather clock ticked against the wall and the house creaked and sighed the way old wooden structures do. Legishon took away their treacle sponges, scarcely touched.

'Let's go outside,' said Pinky, 'greet Africa at night.' They walked to the escarpment edge and stood gazing outwards and upwards.

'Lie flat, Nigel,' said Pinky softly, 'on your back, look at the stars.' Startled, Nigel obeyed.

'Oh,' he said, and 'Oh' again, and reached his hand out and upwards. 'They're at the end of my fingertips, inches away, millions of them, millions and millions of them.'

'Gems on a jeweller's cushion,' said Pinky.

'Diamonds in a velvet sky,' said Nigel. He remained recumbent, adrift in this new world, arms outstretched to grasp the stars.

'Same sky as Eastbourne,' said Pinky matter of factly, 'just no haze here, no smoke, no street lights.'

Looking up at his grandfather, though he could not see him in the inky blackness, Nigel said, 'We're going tomorrow and you haven't finished the story.'

'Story?'

'Magda, Mingati, the house, Mum, England.'

Pinky reached down and pulled the boy to his feet. 'The Equator gets cold at night. There are a couple of skins in an old woodshed if you don't mind the smell of colobus, and a log to sit on.'

* * * * *

Magda went with Pinky because he was kind and he took her away from the expats and their ostentatious pity. Anyway, she was penniless, what else could she do?

'I told myself, she would come to love me,' said Pinky, 'just give her time and space. And so we moved upcountry. Old Charlie Aldington rented a small house to us and a C of E padre married us.'

'Did Min live with you?'

'Good God, no! Min lived the way his tribe always lived – off the land, hunting, always moving. But we had ways to communicate, short or long distances, and when there was work, we would meet up and do the job.'

'Why did Granny hate Min so much?'

'I'm not sure she hated him personally. Yes, he would arrive and I would pick up my guns and leave and she hated that. And yes, she had a sharp tongue and could say some hurtful things but I don't think she seriously questioned us being together. I think for her Mingati embodied everything she feared and distrusted about Africa – friendships, silences and promises, as well as black faces and strange languages. After Charlton, I don't think she could trust again and she hated the place where she had been betrayed and shamed.'

He looked across at the boy's just-visible profile, so like his mother. 'You wouldn't remember your grandma?'

'No, she died before I was born. Mum said she refused to talk about Africa. What really happened, Grandad?'

'What happened was Sonya, our baby, your mother. A born African she was, that little thing, perfect for this country, but Magda was terrified she would come to love it, love it more than her, perhaps. Our hunting safaris were doing better by then and I promised I would build a house for Magda, a magnificent new house, here on the Uplands, the healthiest part of the country, the most beautiful, too.'

'But she left.'

'There had been delays – land permissions, wood supplies, Africa's weather. She said she couldn't live in our hovel – the little rented house – a minute longer. I begged her not to leave, said the house plans were almost ready and it would be hers to name – Magdalena, I thought, would be a wonderful name for a house. I promised to stop hunting and go farming like everyone else. I waited and waited. But she never came back.'

Pinky laughed shortly. 'And the thing was, I kept all the promises. A settler scheme was introduced for war veterans and suddenly I was land-rich and I became a farmer. I built the house and Mingati went back to his tribe to choose a wife.'

'Did you see him again, Mingati?'

'He gave me a gift, it's their tradition when they leave, they leave a gift.'

'What was his gift?'

'His name. He never really understood us Europeans building houses, there was no room in his life for a permanent dwelling, but he knew it meant a lot to me and perhaps one day would to Magda. He turned to me and said in his language, "The House: Mingati." And we embraced and when I accepted that it would never be Magdalena, I called the house Mingati.'

There was a long silence. A greyness had invaded the sky and the stars had gone when Nigel spoke. 'You're going to see him again, aren't you, Grandad, you're going to look for Min?'

Pinky lifted his head. 'His children are long raised, his duties to his people are complete, as are mine. Soon they will ban hunting. A new Africa is coming.'

'But he's there, isn't he, Grandad? Mingati, the hunter, your friend. And you have ways to communicate, you told me. You can signal and he will know it is you. '

Pinky only smiled and as they turned for the house, a roar broke from the tree line. Nigel looked at his grandfather, excited, fearful.

'A lion,' the old man said. 'They sometimes come to the edge of the escarpment, just to make sure everybody knows who is king.'

'Ace,' whispered Nigel, reaching for his grandfather's hand for the first time. 'Magic.'

* * * * *

They had the departure breakfast on the verandah, just fruit for Sonya, eggs and sausages for Pinky, both for Nigel. Suitcases packed and ready to go, Sonya said they would keep the granny flat available for a while since surely her father would change his mind when independence came and the locals took over. Politely, the old man thanked his daughter, then awkwardly embraced his grandson. Nigel pressed his face into the folds of the ancient safari jacket and whispered, 'Don't come to England, Grandad. Get your guns. Go with Min.'

Dry-eyed Sonya was surprised to see tears on the cheeks of both her father and her son.

'Well, you're a couple of softies, I must say,' she joked to hide embarrassment. Then she turned to her father and said lightly, 'Remember Daddy, you're right under the flight path, we'll be over the

Uplands at ten minutes after take-off, so you can look up and wave to Nigel.' Then to everyone's relief, a car horn sounded, Tony Aldington called 'Tally Ho,' and they left for town.

In the sudden quiet, Pinky crossed to the kitchen where Legishon was clearing up the breakfast dishes. Pulling coins from his pocket, he said, 'I won't need you for the rest of the day, Legishon. You did well with the two guests. Here's something extra, take the totos down to the village for a treat.' The cook smiled happily. 'Thank you, Bwana, thank you, maybe we go for the picture show.'

It was evening when Pinky woke. Dusk had settled and the stars were already appearing. The servants' quarters were deserted, everyone down in the village for the ruling party's monthly open-air film show. The old man poured himself a copious brandy, then unlocked his gun safe and ran his fingers across the ordered array of oiled and polished weapons. Finally, he selected a 577 Nitro Express, which he loaded with practised precision. He then sat in his favourite armchair, sipping his cognac with the rifle across his knees.

On the wall directly in front of him was the elephant's head. Pinky looked at it for a long time, then wiped and polished the rifle stock, took careful aim and fired. The explosion, magnified inside the shuttered room, was followed by a smaller one as half of the elephant's skull crashed to the ground. The other half swung from the wall plaque. Pinky reloaded and fired again. This time both the skull and plaque shattered.

Methodically, the old hunter shot his trophies to pieces – only the leopard gave any trouble, one of its glass eyes rebounding like a bullet itself and smashed against Pinky's right hand. 'Typical bloody leopard,' he muttered.

When the heads lay in pieces and the plaques hung askew from the wall, Pinky aimed at the lights of his chandelier, popping them out one by one. He even laughed, pleased by his skill.

By now the downstairs room was lit by only a single table lamp and Pinky walked out through the hall where the lesser trophies hung. This time he did not shoot but taking the butt of his rifle, he smashed it time and again into the head of the wild dog. He then unhooked a bunch of keys from a panel in the hallway and taking a flashlight, unlocked the petrol store. There were five full jerricans inside, he took two and returned to the house.

When he unclipped the seal, his head jerked back at the powerful emanation of vapour. He then began emptying the can around the living room, against the walls, onto the sofa and his favourite armchair; he splashed the liquid across the polished wood dining table and over his books and when the can was empty, he took up the second one.

When his work was done, he stood immobile, breathing shallowly because of the stench and listening to the gurgling sounds as the petrol ran and dripped and spread. He gave it three minutes then reached for a box of matches.

* * * * *

It was 9.00 pm when the airliner climbed from the runway and headed towards northern Africa, the Mediterranean and Europe. Nigel sat in Row 42, Seat F, his face pressed against the window. It was dark and there was little to see, no built-up areas here, no street lighting or advertising signs, just that velvet African blackness.

Then suddenly he straightened, his eye caught by a bright light below. He checked his wrist watch, 9.10 pm, they were directly above Mingati and there it was, his grandfather's signal, a bright, red and white, shape-changing light. 'Look, Min, look,' Nigel whispered, 'your signal! Go to him, Min, he's waiting for you.'

'What's that?' said his mother in the seat next to him.

'Nothing,' said Nigel, turning away as the glare receded. 'It's nothing. Just a light.'

The Frightened Smile

The appointment was for 8 am and Roger got his father to the hospital just about on time. The receptionist pulled up a roster on her computer screen. 'Rodway… Martin Rodway… here it is, *Martin Rodway to see Mr Hirst.*'

'That's right,' said Roger. 'To do with the growth, should be quite quick, I believe.'

'You are Martin Rodway?'

'No, I'm the son.'

She turned to the older man. 'Mr Martin Rodway?'

'Yes, dear, Marty, that's me.'

'Age seventy-four?'

'Seventy-five next week, three-quarters there!'

'Well done!' She smiled. 'Please take a seat. A nurse will be along to talk to you shortly.'

'Have you any idea how long my dad will be here?' asked Roger.

'The nurse will handle that. Just take a seat.' She turned back to her computer.

'Don't give much away do they?' Roger muttered as he and his father took side-by-side seats. 'Plus, they can't even get their own schedules right.' He pointed to a flickering screen headed "Department Schedules, June 18", two days earlier.

'I can't read that,' said Martin, peering. 'Anyway, why? Do you have somewhere to go?'

Roger shrugged. 'I just don't want to waste all day sitting here.'

Martin picked up a *National Geographic* and leafed through the pages, squinting and holding the wildlife photos sideways to catch the light.

It was 8.45 when Nurse Bright appeared.

'Mr Rodway? Please come with me. And you, sir? You are…?'

'… Roger Rodway, his son. They said it would be an in-and-out affair.'

'First to my office, please, a bit of weighing and measuring and I'll explain.'

The nurse checked her screen. 'Right, Mr Rodway, what we're planning is an elliptical excision. Mr Hirst will remove the lesion from your neck that has been giving you so much trouble. Usually the wound closes very neatly but because of your age, the surgeon might decide to do a skin graft.'

'Nobody mentioned that,' said Roger. 'Is that a lengthy procedure?'

'Not at all,' said the nurse. 'If he chooses that option, Mr Hirst will take a small portion of skin probably from behind the ear and stretch it over the wound.'

'Done with a local anaesthetic, not the general knock-out?' asked Roger.

'That's right. But of course, your father will have to be gowned and fully prepped. The procedure itself takes place in the operating theatre with a full team and all necessary backup. And then he must rest afterwards so we can be sure he is well enough to leave.'

'But he will be out today?'

She turned away and spoke to Martin. 'We have to weigh and measure you, check on your current medication, then get you gowned.'

Martin pretended to shiver. 'One of those draughty-down-the-back hospital gowns?'

'Afraid so, sir, but you can pop your overcoat on while you're waiting.'

Back in the public area, Roger picked up his father's magazine and flicked through the pages without looking at them. 'It's always the same, isn't it? Hurry up and stand still. Bloody health service! Wouldn't be like this in the States.'

Martin did not seem to hear.

Roger turned back to him. 'Dad, did you give any thought to that thing I mentioned?'

'What thing, son?'

'You know, the bond?'

'Oh, the bond.'

'The Excelsior bond. The five-year term is up and you can cash it in now. It would be nice for you to have that money available.'

'I don't know, Roger, I might decide to reinvest it.'

Roger stared. 'What! Another five years at your age!'

Martin sighed. 'You were never known for your sensitivity, were you, Roger?'

'Sorry Dad, I didn't mean anything. It just seems … I mean, forty thousand locked up like that, doing nothing, going nowhere...'

Martin lowered his voice. 'How did you know about it anyway, Roger, the bond?'

'You told me, Dad, don't you remember, the time I had that bit business trouble? You said I should keep an eye on expiry dates and so-on.'

'I don't remember. I know I cashed in ten thousand to help you out.' He paused. 'But, you could be right, son, I'm forgetful these days.'

'I can get the paperwork done for encashment, Dad. It will be no problem, all you'd have to do is sign. What say? Shall I go ahead?'

Before Martin could answer, a brown-coated auxiliary nurse beckoned them to a changing room. Patient's weight, height and medication confirmed, they took seats in the pre-op area among others in gowns and robes sitting anxiously with their relatives.

'How long will all this take?' Roger asked. The auxiliary consulted a clipboard.

'Mr Rodway is fourth on Mr Hirst's list, so he should be taken down in about an hour. Then there's the surgery and then a mandatory rest and check-up.'

'Ouch! So it could be afternoon?'

'We have no way of knowing precisely how long an operation will take, sir, and we must do things properly. This is an oncology unit.'

Roger wandered to the exit and joined a group of smokers. He took a light from a pyjama-clad patient who had a cigarette in one hand and his mobile drip in the other. Together they watched ambulances come and go.

Ten minutes later, pocketing his pack of ten, Roger said, 'Dad, I really have something to do. Would you mind if I popped out for a bit? I'd just be sitting here like a dummy anyway.'

'How will you know when I get out, Roger?'

'My mobile, of course. I'll keep checking.'

'OK, son, but be sure to come and collect me after and take me home.'

'Dad, come on! Do you think I'd forget about you?'

* * * * *

It took Martin two minutes, maybe three, to answer the door these days, but Mrs Maltby knew that and waited patiently with her fresh-baked cake until the door chain rattled and her neighbour appeared.

'Just a little morale booster, Marty,' she said, 'after your trials yesterday. I thought you should pamper yourself a bit.'

Martin Rodway beamed. 'Oh, how kind, Mrs Maltby, come in, come in and share it with me and we can chat.'

It was a coconut cake, Martin noticed, knowing the fragments would get under his dentures, but that would never occur to Mrs Maltby. What she was good at was spotting nuances and upsets, those minute vibrations in life that did not ring quite true.

Over tea and cake, she mined Martin's day at the hospital. He showed her the dressings on his neck and behind his ear, explained the skin graft procedure and stressed the hospital's assurances that he would get no more pain from the lesion. When she asked how long they had been there, he tried to fudge Roger's long absence but Mrs Maltby spotted the evasion. 'You mean he left you sitting there alone? All gowned and prepared? For an hour before your operation? Marty, that's outrageous.'

'He said he had something on the go and there was no point in hanging around, there was nothing he could do.'

'Probably off on another of his get-rich-quick schemes with his American pals. They never seem to work though, do they?'

Roger had returned to the ward late, but Martin didn't protest because the operation had exhausted him. The surgery itself was just a tickly sensation in the neck, but it hurt when the anaesthesia wore off. He stumbled badly as they helped him back into the wheelchair, and he needed the sick basin for a while. But there had been no real pain and then Roger was there and they were on their way home.

'They want to check me in a day or two but they will send out a nurse for that and the doctor said I should be in great shape to celebrate my 75th on Tuesday.'

'So what are you planning?' asked Mrs Maltby.

The old man hesitated. 'Well, I wanted a nice meal here at home – you, the Millers over the road, my church friends and of course Roger and his new girl. I think you can get food delivered these days and I'm sure you would have contributed one of your delicacies.'

'Of course, but what …?'

'Roger thinks a meal out would be better. Less taxing for me, less organisation, no fuss. Just him and Chayenne and me at a restaurant in town.'

Mrs Maltby glared. 'Which Roger would choose and where you would pay!'

'It's not that so much, I just don't feel comfortable eating in public any more, my teeth you know.'

'Marty, that's awful. I've a good mind to call that Roger and tell him the things that you won't.'

'Please don't, Mrs Maltby, Roger has been unlucky with some business ventures but his heart's in the right place and he says he hasn't been too well lately.'

'Rubbish! Excuses! Marty, I know I have no right to poke my nose in. But do be careful with that boy.' She paused. 'He hasn't been asking for money again, has he?'

Martin looked away. 'He thinks a French restaurant would be best, especially for me with my knowledge of France.'

'Your knowledge of France? You've never been to France.'

'Oh yes, I was a tourist there. Twice. That was Roger's little joke. Dunkirk in 1940 and Normandy 1944.'

'Very funny.' Mrs Maltby said, but she did not laugh.

* * * * *

La Grenouille was new, but Roger said the food was good, he knew the maître d' personally and he had booked a private banquette. The maître looked taken aback by Roger's effusive greeting – 'René, bonjour mon ami, c'est, c'est – it's so nice to see you again' – but he smiled amiably at Martin and Chayenne and led them all to a table ten paces from the kitchen.

Roger shook his head at that. 'I thought the guy taking the booking had dodgy English, looks like he got it wrong.' He lowered his voice. 'Bloody Frogs. The Yanks wouldn't screw up like that.'

Roger insisted on Kirs all round as Martin scanned the menu, not for his favourites but for dishes he could eat without embarrassment. So no soup to betray his shaky hands and no steak that would defeat his sliding dentures. He declined a starter and ordered grilled lemon sole with new potatoes. Roger asked for oysters and a minute steak and Chayenne pointed to moules mariniere and cassoulet.

Roger was sawing energetically at his steak when he returned to the Excelsior bond. 'Liquidity is important, Dad, what with the recession and all. Good to have something substantial in the bank rather than tied up and inaccessible for years. It's all your money of course, in your own account, only available with your say-so. Know what I mean?'

Martin shot an embarrassed look at Chayenne. 'Oh she's fine,' said Roger, 'she's almost family. Aren't you darling? You don't mind us talking finance, do you?' Chayenne, tall, blonde and well-upholstered like all Roger's lady friends, looked up from her stew. 'Course not, silly, I probably wouldn't understand it anyway.'

The fish was excellent but Martin put his knife and fork down and looked across the table. 'So what is it this time, Roger? Seed money for a real estate business in expanding Toledo? A spot of capital for "Posh Nosh, the Caff Where the Brits Eat" in Brooklyn? Or money to oil the wheels of an import-export deal where the only export is my cash into your pocket?'

'Now don't be like that, Dad. You know they were mostly good ideas, you said so yourself. I just seemed to get involved with the wrong people.'

Martin nodded. 'You're right there, Roger, your judgment of people has never been the best.'

Roger spoke slowly. 'Actually, Dad, it's a bit more serious than that.'

'Oh dear. What is it, Roger?'

'That last business in New York, they're saying I owe them. I don't really but they're pressing me. They want me to come in on a foot spa business, you know where ladies let fish nibble their toes.'

'Good grief, Roger.'

'Dad, it's all the rage and the location they identified is perfect – a commuter town full of bored, New York-obsessed females aspiring to the latest in beauty treatment.'

'Are you being threatened, Roger?'

'Not threatened, Dad, but they'll forget about our past, er, differences if I agree to invest in the foot spa. Not threats really, more pressure. Yes, pressure … '

Roger faltered and lowered his head. Chayenne was looking hard at him. 'You all right, sweetheart? You're looking pale again.'

'Probably the oysters,' Roger said. 'I'll just clear my head.' He walked unsteadily outside.

'That's the second time he's been like that lately,' Chayenne told Martin. 'He should be more careful. It's not everybody who can take sea food.'

'I don't recall him being allergic,' said Martin.

He repeated the remark when Roger returned, smiling weakly. 'No, not allergic, but I believe you can react differently as your body changes. I'm fine now, a ciggy and a breath of fresh air do wonders.'

He took his seat again and looked hopefully at Martin. 'About that other then, Dad, what do you think?'

'Bring the paperwork over Thursday afternoon, son, and we'll get this thing done. I hope this one works. I'm about emptied out now.'

Roger and Chayenne embraced the older man enthusiastically and wished him a happy birthday. And Roger did not protest too hard when Martin picked up the bill.

* * * * *

The birthday dinner was a month-old memory when father and son met in Martin's house at 7 am. The taxi was due in twenty minutes.

'How was America, Roger?' Martin asked. 'I'm still not sure what you did over there.'

'Oh, all the usual stuff Dad, don't worry, everything went fine. I put my whack into the nibbling fish venture and that was a relief to them.' He laughed nervously. 'And to me.'

'Not the whole forty thousand?'

'No, no, Dad, just enough to keep everybody happy.'

'So you still have the rest? What, twenty, thirty?'

'Well actually, I needed funds for something else, in LA.'

'God, Roger, no.'

'This was different, Dad. A very reputable physician, Doctor Aaron Bronson, runs a top-level practice investigating chronic physical complaints which defy orthodox treatment.'

'You don't need to go on, Rodge… the doctor needed investors… just twenty grand or so to ensure supplies of a magic powder ground from the bark of a tree found only in the African jungle … the results will astound the world… you will make millions…'

'Don't be sarcastic Dad, you're no good at it, and no, it wasn't like that at all.'

The taxi hooted outside and Roger broke off. 'I'll tell you when we get there.'

* * * * *

The appointment was for 8 am and the taxi got them there just about on time. The nurse at reception pulled up a roster on her computer screen. 'Rodway… Roger Rodway… here it is, *Roger Rodway to see Mr Hirst for consultation.*'

'That's right,' said Martin.

'You are Roger Rodway?'

'No, I'm Martin, his father.'

She turned to the younger man. 'Mr Roger Rodway?'

'RR Esquire at your service,' said Roger.

'Please take a seat. A nurse will talk to you shortly.'

Martin turned to Roger. 'Rodge, you've told me nothing about this health problem. Is it serious? Is it what I've got? Why are we in oncology?'

'Seriously Dad, I don't know. They didn't know in America either. Dad, that was what the other twenty went on. I wasn't an investor in Dr Bronson's medical practice, I was a patient.'

Martin stared. 'Oh God, Roger, I'm sorry, I didn't guess.' He reached for his son's hand. 'But Rodge, we've got a perfectly good health service here, and it's free.'

'Free maybe, but perfectly good? Not like the Yanks, Dad. I got hours and hours of personal attention, from the best medical minds in the business.'

'But they didn't cure you, Roger! They didn't even find out what you've got! You threw away twenty thousand on a bunch of millionaire quacks. And you wasted precious time when the doctors here could have been saving your life.'

'Steady on Dad, that's a bit dramatic.'

Martin looked around and lowered his voice. 'So where do you stand exactly? You took tests last week. And you are going to get the results now?'

'The initial results pointed to a possible oncological problem, but only possible, very unaggressive – just like you, Dad, unaggressive.' Martin did not laugh and Roger went on, 'The Hirst guy will have studied the results and will now prescribe treatment – medication of some sort, probably tablets, maybe a scan will be needed.'

'Or surgery or radiation or chemo!'

'Come on, Dad, please.'

'Roger, I wish you'd told me.'

A nurse with a clipboard called out, 'Mr Roger Rodway?'

'At your service, ma'am,' said Roger.

Martin stood. 'I'm his father.' But the nurse held up a hand. 'Sorry, only the patient at the first consultation. We'll call you in later, of course. Please take a seat. A tea trolley will be coming round.'

Roger turned his head as he walked away, smiling that frightened, uncertain smile that wrenched his father's heart. 'You will be here when I get out, Dad?'

Martin nodded and smiled back, trying hard to hide his tears.

From Mummy, With Love

Jane Parks (japark21@gromail.com)
To: Juliette

To my darling daughter the honour of my First Email!! Do confirm you received it, sweetheart, I will feel so pleased with myself! And thank young Tom for setting me up with the laptop and explaining The System. What a clever young man he is! He will be back at college now (Uni he calls it!) but he didn't give me his email address, so be sure and give him a kiss from his old gran.

These emails are wonderful. I am asking my friends for their details when I see them but I haven't had too many responses. But computers are not really the thing with old ladies, are they? Nor, in Little Sutton, old men either, it seems. I suppose I'm ahead of the field there! (Modesty prevents me from adding, Not for the first time!)

Oh yes, nearly forgot – I think Rose Cottage may have been sold. From my side bedroom window, I could see unusual activity yesterday. Estate agents, I dare say, though there was an elderly man, who just might be my new neighbour! Needless to say, I'm keeping a sharp lookout.

Love from Mummy.

Jane Parks (japark21@gromail.com)
To: Juliette

So I did it right! Thank you Julie for confirming my email arrived.

How exciting! As Tom said, I am 'up and running.' My arthritic old fingers are a bit stiff but the computer makes it easy to correct errors.

Busy day yesterday: Post Office for pension in the morning (that Mrs Jordan really needs to do something about her BO, and her a public servant! I think someone should have a quiet word with her about it), then to St Nectan's for tea and cakes with the vicar and the ladies. Plans for the Jubilee coming on apace, (despite losing Reverend Nicholson's attention occasionally as it strayed towards young Mrs Jones' hemline!) She's a newcomer, recently bereaved according to report. Some people think she is pretty.

Rose Cottage is confirmed sold! After all these months! New owner said to be a retired gentleman. Probably the one I spotted, though he looked a bit, I don't know, raffish. I'll be watching.

Mum.

Jane Parks (japark21@gromail.com)
To Juliette

No Julie, relax! I have NO INTENTION of being the one to advise Mrs Jordan about her pong. Whatever made you think I would? I just feel in a village like ours where we live virtually in each other's pockets, we should all be concerned for the comfort of our neighbours.

I have stopped dropping my letters into the box at the Post Office. I am just not comfortable with one villager knowing all about the correspondence activities of another villager. So now I use the box at the far end of the village, it's emptied by the postman who comes in his van.

Another Jubilee meeting, supposedly about fund-raising, but we didn't get far, probably because the vicar wasn't there. 'Sent apologies,' Miss Spennymoor said. I couldn't help noticing that the young widow wasn't there either.

My new neighbour is indeed the raffish elderly gentleman I spotted. No sign of a Mrs Raffish. Seems his things were moved in when I was at the church meeting, pity. I was thinking about introducing myself, perhaps baking a cake. But that's a bit American isn't it? I also thought he might knock on my door. He's a newcomer and I could ease him into village life with introductions and so on. Well, up to him.

And here's a FIRST! A coloured gentleman in Little Sutton! No, not a new resident, gracious no, a workman from Great Sutton, odd job man – THAT was hastily established! He repaired the wonky counter at the Post Office, and not before time, I may say. (Incidentally, I now stand back when I'm anywhere near Mrs Jordan, do you think she HAS something?) Anyway, the black man was in no hurry to depart, still there talking to Mrs J and drinking tea when I came back from putting flowers on your dad's grave. The BO doesn't seem to bother him, but then it wouldn't, would it, him being from Africa!

Tom said he would send me an email and I could pick up his address from that, but nothing so far.

Mumsy.

Jane Parks (japark21@gromail.com)
To Juliette

Julie, hello. I'm a bit surprised I have not garnered more email contacts. I know quite a few villagers are online, as they say, but I've only had promises so far. Miss Spennymoor did say she hardly ever uses her computer, which surprised me, her being a teacher all her life.

The black gentleman was back again, working in the store room, Mrs J said. I could certainly hear banging from the back but that could have been anything, couldn't it? I did ask, just offhand, if her husband was involved in such decisions. She gave me one of her looks, said Jack was perfectly happy for her to run the Post Office, thank you, he had enough to worry about out there on the rigs. Oops, sorry I asked.

I'm slightly, just slightly, concerned about Neighbour Raffish with the long hair. Last night a young boy went up the path and knocked and he let him in and the evening before that, it was another boy. That one had a briefcase. Just wondering, you know, with all that stuff about the Catholics. Not that he's a priest or anything. But no sign of a lady wife. I wonder if Sergeant Lacey knows about the boys. Somebody should tell him and he could make a discreet check.

Yr loving Mum.

Jane Parks (japark21@gromail.com)
To Juliette

Julie, really, dear, I am NOT Interfering in people's lives and I am NOT making unwarranted assumptions. And a little bit unfair of you to bring up that thing from long ago. I explained all that to you when you were old enough. As you know, I have always had a lively curiosity and despite my age, that has not diminished. I am just concerned for what's best for the village. I needn't remind you I have lived here all my life, though you and your brother seem not to have shared my affection for your birthplace since you couldn't get away fast enough, the both of you.

But not to quarrel. Not much to tell from Little S, except I finally met with my neighbour. He was just leaving the cottage as I was closing my front door, pure coincidence. His name is Smyth. 'With a y but no e,' he said. I must have looked blank. Then he spelled it: SMYTH, pronounced Smith. (A bit pretentious?) I said, 'Welcome to Little Sutton, Mr Smyth,' but I can't pretend it was the warmest greeting in the world. I did not refer to the boys but I have reason to think the sergeant might be checking soon and that would put my mind at rest.

Bye, love.

Jane Parks (japarks21@gromail.com)
To Juliette

As you suggested, I have been spending more time in my garden. The pansies look lovely around the cherry tree and the tree is heavy with blossom again. What a generous fruiter it is! I'll be watching for the little green nodules, soon to turn pink and red – just need to be sure I get to them before the blackbirds!

I can't ignore village life entirely, however, and as a committee member for St Nectan's Jubilee, I am required to attend the fortnightly planning meeting in the vestry. Once again our vicar and Mrs Jones were absent. I know the lady is widowed but he is SO much older than her. I suggested sotto voce that it was becoming an open scandal but none of the other ladies seemed to hear me. I wonder if the Bishop knows.

With Easter approaching, I want to brush up my Easter card list. But when I asked Mrs Jordan for her husband's address, she gave me another of her looks and wanted to know WHY. To send him an Easter card, I said, I send everyone Easter cards, what's wrong with that? She didn't even reply, just turned away. How rude! I suppose his employers would forward a message to him.

Julie, are you serious about going to live in Australia? Tom would be all on his own. Tom Senior feeling homesick, is he?

Mum.

Jane Parks (japarks21@gromail.com)
To Juliette

Julie, you were so angry on your telephone call I don't think you were listening to me. I am very sorry Sergeant Lacey called you. He had no business doing that. The whole thing was a big misunderstanding and I could easily have told you myself. And asking you to "have a word" with me, your own mother, really! What happened is he called at Rose Cottage and he was inside quite a long time. When he emerged, they shook hands and stared openly at my bedroom window, then the sergeant knocked on my door. He told me my suspicions were unwarranted – Mr Smyth is a music teacher, piano and clarinet, and the boys are his students. Well, how was I to know? The sergeant talked about offences under the Communications Act or something, harassment, hate mail, anonymous letters and so on. Of course, he knows all about that business in the past so I'm a natural target, I suppose. I said sorry, I had acted with the best of intentions. He said I should be happy Mr Smyth did not wish to take the matter further but I should consider his visit an official warning. As if I was a ten-year-old schoolgirl instead of a conscientious woman doing her duty! The whole thing has upset me terribly.

The other thing that upset me was when you said you definitely decided to emigrate to Australia. I will of course soldier on here, as I always have, and there is always Tom, though will he not go, too, when he has his degree? Life can be very lonely for an old lady these days. Do come and see me so we can talk it all through and make peace.

Mother.

Jane Parks (japark21@gromail.com)
To Juliette

So Tom has been offered an internship in Melbourne when he graduates. Well, good luck to the boy, he has his future ahead of him, unlike me.
I called on Doctor Curry the other day. My arthritis is worsening and all this talk of police has upset me greatly, I have stomach pains and at night I just toss and turn. He prescribed sleeping pills but I have no confidence in him. Young doctors have fresh ideas. With Doc Curry, it's the same old thing.

Do you have a date for your departure? Will you be coming to Little Sutton to see me before you go?

I love you, Julie.

Your devoted mother.

Jane Parks (japark21@gromail.com)
To Juliette

Julie, I was so pleased to see you when you arrived, even if it was your farewell before Australia, but then to quarrel as we did! Just because I mentioned Mrs Jordan and the young widow.

Julie, you said you would not be in contact with me again. I am sure you said this in anger – we all know that hot temper of yours! Julie, if you cast me off it would be a most unChristian thing to do and I did not bring you up that way. I am a defenceless old woman and Miss Spennymoor has been hinting that I should leave the Jubilee committee because of the walk and my bad knee – just excuses to offload me, of course. Here alone without you to turn to would quite break my heart, and Tom never did give me his email address.

Mummy

Jane Parks (japark21@gromail.com)
To Juliette

Three weeks now and I still haven't heard from you. I know how stubborn you can be, Julie. But that goes for me, too, and I have decided I will keep sending you emails anyway and perhaps when you are quite settled in Australia and over your anger, you will get back in touch.

The pansies are finished, even the daffs, but the cherries are coming into their own. I was thinking of giving some to my neighbour, a kind of peace offering – no fruit trees in Rose Cottage garden. But he does not speak when we pass.

The Jubilee garden fête seemed to be a big success. They got a wonderful day, weatherwise. Not that I was there, but I did happen to walk past the church field and there were a lot of stalls and lots of visitors. I could have helped out, of course, a pair of willing hands, but that's all water under the bridge now.

Your mum (despite everything.)

Jane Parks (japark21@gmail.com)
To Juliette

You will have noticed I don't email you so often, Julie. Nothing much to say, for one thing, and one-way communication is frustrating. Has young Tom joined you over there? By my calculation his results will be out. I thought he might email me, I'm sure he did well, but nothing.

Big rumour here is that we are losing the post office. They are closing down all the small ones. If it's true, Mrs J and her BO (oops sorry) will be gone (plus the African gentleman, I imagine) but I will have to take the bus to Great Sutton for my pension. I could get it paid into my bank account but I have always enjoyed the human contact.

Do let me know how you are doing. Don't be hard, Juliette.

Mum

Jane Parks (japark21@gromail.com)
To Juliette

I was quite excited the other day when a caravan drew up down Garden Lane. I decided to stroll past, despite my dodgy knee. I was sure they were Gyppos and we don't want any of their sort. But they were just ordinary trippers en route to the coast. They sat on their little canvas stools and ate sandwiches, then drove off again. End of excitement!

They say we are in for a hard winter. I'm not looking forward to it, these old cottages are hard to keep warm.

I thought I might hear from you on my birthday, a phone call perhaps. Nothing from Tom, either, after all those years when his granny sent him birthday cards faithfully, not a year missed. The question is: How many more birthdays will I have?

As ever, Mumsy.

Jane Parks (japark21@hotmail.com)
To Juliette

Bad news, Julie! It's about those pains. Dr Curry would not come out and be specific, but I have been given a date for hospital admission 'for investigation,' and I think we both can guess what the biopsies will tell us. I can't help thinking about your grandmother. I fear it's in the family.

Julie, believe me, this is the truth I am telling you. But then again, you have been silent so long, you may be dead yourself for all I know. Or moved on to Africa or somewhere, and I'm just talking to myself.

Anyway, you have my telephone number, that hasn't changed. One way or another I'm sure we will be in touch again.

Mum.

Jane Parks (japark21@hotmail.com)
To Juliette

I am dictating this to a kind nurse, Sister Olga, to keep you informed. I had exploratory surgery and without going into detail, the news is not good. The doctors are conferring on the next step but as I always say, where there's life, there's hope! The only thing is I am very tired.

--- OO ---

Mrs Newhouse, I have sent the message above in your mother's own words since she can no longer manage the computer. Officially, I am sorry to tell you that the prospects for your mother's recovery are negligible. This hospital, the Royal George in Great Sutton, requires that as next of kin you should contact us immediately for necessary official arrangements. Thank you. Your mother asks me to add, 'Julie, I love you.' – Sister Olga Miller.

When Molly Turned Into Mary

Everybody was deeply shocked, though myself, I knew nothing about it. One moment I was heading down the street to Tesco's with my wheelie bag, the next I was waking up in a hospital bed, having been unconscious for three weeks.

A fall and a knock on the head? A stroke? A virus? A catastrophic drop in blood pressure? Something genetic? I never heard so many theories, or was asked so many questions. Scans, X-rays, jabs … I had them all and still they haven't given me an explanation. It's the memory loss that engages the specialists; as for the nurses, they are fascinated, even frightened you might say, by my behaviour and attitude. Of course, I know what upsets them.

It was the middle of the afternoon when I returned to the land of the living. I heard a man's voice, from far away it seemed but urgent, calling, 'Nurse, nurse,' then a nurse leaning over me, speaking softly, comforting. 'You're all right now, love,' she kept saying, 'just relax and lean back, you've been away a long time.' The light was bright over her shoulder and I heard scurrying footsteps, whispers about the duty doctor. Somebody guided a drinking straw between my lips. Slowly my vision cleared and figures came into focus, including a man at the foot of the bed, the one who called for the nurse, I assumed.

He took my hand with obvious affection. 'Molly, Molly, we wondered if you would ever come back to us.' He kissed my knuckles. I withdrew my hand sharply. He looked concerned.

'Who are you?' I asked.

'Molly, come on, it's me, Andrew, your husband.' His voice faltered when I did not respond. 'Andy,' he tried to joke, 'the father of our girls ...'

I squinted at him, puzzled, silent. I did not remember him. Not for one moment, not in any sense. He was a total stranger.

He looked stricken, glanced in appeal at the nurse, who said. 'Don't press her, let her take her time.'

But I knew it would make no difference. Not only did I not know him, I did not like him and I knew I never would. I did not like his pointed nose and thinning hair nor his ingratiating smile and I hated his mustard coloured suit. He had a smudge of shaving foam on his ear and I hated that, too.

* * * * *

Those early, post-coma days are a muddle. My body had wasted, my hair was stringy and lifeless and my skin was papery and pale. It was quickly acknowledged that I had lost my memory on a comprehensive basis – after all, I did not know my husband – but there was much optimism that this would return with patience and therapy. So when suddenly I declared, 'Here is Mr Logan' at the sight of my specialist, the medics were amazed and delighted and "selective memory loss" became the mantra much heard around my bed. I had not forgotten everybody.

Through the subsequent days of recuperation, though I remembered everything that happened after I regained consciousness, it became obvious that whatever synapses controlled my past were out of control. Names were put to me of neighbours, shopkeepers, public officials, the prime minister; some of these were people I scarcely knew, yet I remembered them perfectly, while others, relatives and close friends, were a closed book, including my husband and one of our two daughters.

The tests and the therapy were aimed at filling in the blanks, but while my body began its journey back to normal, or whatever was normal for a 66-year-old woman, the mind refused to co-operate and I won back no single aspect of those who had become strangers. Importantly, this involved the man who sat by my bed every day in what became a trial for both of us. I saw the hopeful expectation in his eyes each time he arrived and the puzzlement that replaced it as he detected my unresponsive gaze. He talked hopefully of our life together, our first meeting at the rowing club, our blossoming love, marriage, two lost children before two fine girls, their own marriages, their children, their moves away. I remembered none of it. After two hours, Andrew would smile one more time, a brush of the lips, 'Goodbye my love, see you tomorrow,' and go on his way, an elderly, stooping, unhappy man.

In time, I detected, if not a hostility, then a growing hardness in the nurses' attitude to me. I did not blame them. Andrew's daily humiliation at my bedside must have been hard for them to watch, but what could I do? I did not know, much less love this man whose hopes for my transformation were doomed to defeat. I might have pretended or play-acted, of course, but this was not in my nature and meanwhile a greater darkness overlaid my response – the prospect of returning to live in intimacy in this man's house.

* * * * *

It was six weeks after emerging from the coma that Mr Logan decided my physical rehabilitation was complete and if the restoration of my lost memories was less than successful, therapy could continue on an outpatient basis or with the therapists visiting me at home. And home was somewhere I remembered perfectly, the stone-fronted Victorian terrace house in the inner suburb with the high-ceilinged bedrooms and the long, steep staircases. I just could not picture Andrew in it. I had dissuaded him from coming with me in the ambulance, but I knew without doubt that he would be waiting on the doorstep with some effusive ceremonial. There was no "Welcome Home, Molly" banner decorating the outside of the house as I feared, but everything else suggested the arrival of the Queen of Sheba: a bouquet of flowers pressed into my arms and a basket of fruit on the hall table as if I was a VIP guest at some third-rate hotel, an assortment of greetings cards and a large toy panda in my old armchair (here it was *his* memory that was at fault, I had always loathed the sentimentality of adult toys and this he had forgotten).

Having escorted me to the armchair by the fire, Andrew dithered between the living room and the kitchen. I saw preparations in train for a full-scale meal.

'No, Andrew,' I said, 'no, no, just some tea and biscuits.' His face tautened once more before he chirped, 'So be it, Molly, char and biccies coming up!'

'And I want black tea, not that milky stuff.'

'You take your tea black now, do you? Fine, Molly, fine, black tea it is.'

'And one more thing. No more Molly, please. My proper name is Mary. So Mary, please, from now on!'

What a bitch I sounded. How often every day, I wondered, did I disappoint this man whom I could not love? By the time I left the hospital, the nurses had become markedly cool towards me. I had even heard a muttered "hard-faced cow." And I had one more major disappointment for brave and loyal Andrew.

'You'll love our bedroom,' he said, bending over me, but not touching. He did not touch me as often now. 'I had it re-papered and painted and got all new bed linen. It's really beautiful.'

'Sorry, Andrew,' I said, and judging by his troubled features he knew what was coming. 'Not *our* bedroom. Mine or yours. Please understand, my memory has not returned. All I know of you is what I've heard. I do not want to hurt you, but I cannot share a room, much less a bed, with a stranger.'

'That's fine, fine, fine,' he interrupted, 'whatever you decide. Perhaps later…' He paused and unusually, his eyes stayed on me as the unspoken question hung in the air. The anxious look was gone. It was as if he had made a decision. He's accepted me, I thought, me, Mary. Then he turned away and so life restarted at 6 Edenvale Terrace: Two people in the same house, separate entities, one stony, unsmiling, the other looking, searching and waiting for a sign that never came.

* * * * *

We had lived like this for two months, when the daughter I did remember, Francie, shook off the responsibilities of a grand job and came to stay for a day or two. Andrew told Francie how much better I was getting, how lucky we were that he had retired in time to look after us both, how excellent were the therapists who refused to give up on my memory problems, how he was sure the old Molly would soon be back.

'But you sleep in separate bedrooms,' Francie said. Francie never dodged an issue.

'Oh, that's just temporary,' said Andrew, 'till Mom adjusts.'

'Temporary? After two months?'

She looked at me. I said nothing and the little inquest petered out in embarrassment. But I knew it was not over. Sure enough, next day, the day before she was leaving, she sat me down while Andrew was out shopping. 'Why, Mom, why?' she asked. 'You're crushing Daddy. Can't you see the pain he is in … his stoicism, that face he puts on – *everything will be all right, give her time?* Don't you see it?'

She was right, I knew, and of course I did see it. I did not wish to cause my husband pain, but I was never a role-player. When I came out of the coma, I actively disliked him. I had suppressed that dislike. I could do no more.

'I am thinking of seeing a lawyer about a divorce,' I said.

Francie was shocked. 'No, Mom, please, that would kill him.'

'Living a lie is killing me.'

'But losing you is his worst nightmare. I know sometimes he has been overbearing, controlling even, always the one to decide and your new "character" is a challenge to him, from a mouse to a lion! But he has always been fearful of your leaving him for someone else, of making a bolt for independence. You know his insecurity, his fears over the years.'

'Francie, I do NOT know. This is a person of whom I have no recollection, remember? How he feels now I can deduce from his behaviour, his looks. But what happened in the past I do NOT know, believe me. I do not even know what I myself was like. Don't you understand? As for somebody else, that's nonsense. I'm an elderly woman, I have no suitors, I want my freedom, that's all.'

The argument went back and forth. 'Many married people grow up and grow apart,' Francie argued. 'They live single lives in a kind of partnership. Think about that. There must be a solution.'

We agreed not to mention anything to Andrew yet and Francie left the next day.

That night in my large, redecorated, sweet-smelling bedroom – my husband had moved into the second of the house's four bedrooms across the corridor – my mind nagged at my dilemma. I could no longer live in this house with Andrew, that was fact. And since clearly I could not leave, then he must go, either voluntarily or under the terms of a divorce arrangement. But he could be stubborn, that I had already detected, and hard, too, I suspected, and he might easily defy any court order to quit. I could just imagine him declaring in that half-jokey, half-serious tone he sometimes adopted, "They will have to carry me out of here in a box."

* * * * *

The inquest was not held for many weeks. But as the loving husband of Mary Sylvia Bridges, I was kept informed about the investigation by the Coroner's Officer, a kindly lady who said a post-mortem was necessary because of my late wife's unexplained collapse those many months before and because of the circumstances of her sudden demise.

Also because (though she did not realise I had overheard this) 'a lot of old people seem to be falling downstairs these days.'

I was the first witness. I said it was the middle of the night when I heard a bump and a cry, then a series of loud thuds. I found my dear wife in her nightdress spread-eagled near the bottom of the stairs. I knew she was dead right away from the impossible angle of her head. I said my wife sometimes rose in the night to use the bathroom and would have needed to cross the top of the staircase. I said we had planned to turn her bedroom into an en suite arrangement but that had not yet been done. The Coroner asked about my feelings for my wife. I assured him I loved Molly deeply and though my wife had memory problems after her collapse on the street, I was sure she loved me, too.

The ambulance man who answered my 999 call testified that my wife showed no vital signs and the policeman who came soon after corroborated this.

The pathologist declared that internal investigation revealed no problem with the heart of the deceased and the cause of death, in layman's terms, was a broken neck. Finally, Mr Logan outlined Molly's past collapse, its circumstances and his unsuccessful efforts to diagnose a cause. When the Coroner asked if such a collapse could have happened again, Mr Logan said that was entirely possible. Accordingly, with appropriate expressions of sympathy, the Coroner passed a verdict of Accidental Death, expressing the opinion that Mrs Bridges had most likely suffered a repeat collapse, unfortunately at the top of a long staircase, the most dangerous spot in the house.

* * * * *

Francie drove me home in silence. At the foot of the staircase where Molly had ended her life, she turned to me:

'You knew, didn't you?'

'What? Knew what?'

'You knew she planned to divorce you. You came back early when we were talking about it and you listened in the kitchen.'

I stretched my hand out. 'Francie, now...'

'Don't Francie me,' she said furiously. 'You could not bear her getting away from you, out of your control, the way it always is with you. You couldn't bear it that she had stopped admiring you, idolising you like your little handmaiden from the past, that the collapse had changed her character.'

'I loved your mother, Francie. How can you accuse me of hurting her?'

'I don't mean you pushed her down the stairs, you are too subtle for that.' She paused, then: 'Daddy, there was a small foot mat at the head of the stairs on that little landing. I noticed it when I stayed with you. I thought then it was lethal, a death trap. Where is it? What happened to it?'

I pondered. 'That old thing? I threw it out. You're right, it was dangerous. It could skid away from your feet.'

'Especially if the grips were removed and it was treated with a spot of polish. Or soap. Or butter would do.'

'The police examined everything, Francie, the landing in particular. She collapsed at the top of the stairs. The Coroner said so.'

My daughter turned away without a word. I heard her car door slam and the engine roar and she drove out of my life.

In the kitchen I made myself a cup of tea, sweet and milky the way Molly really liked it. In the centre of the kitchen table was a folding photo frame, with on one side a picture of my wife taken long ago, smiling shyly, and opposite a snap I took on the day she arrived home, serious and staring straight at the camera. I slipped this last photo out of the frame and tore it into pieces, then I put the frame with its remaining photo back in the centre of the table.

'There you go, Molly,' I whispered, 'you're my girl again. Dear, dear Molly.'

IRON Press is among the country's longest established independent literary publishers.
The press began operations in 1973 with IRON Magazine which ran for 83 editions until 1997. Since 1975 we have also brought out a regular list of individual collections of poetry, fiction and drama plus various anthologies ranging from *The Poetry of Perestroika*, through *Limerick Nation*, *100 Island Poems* and *Cold Iron, Ghost Stories from the 21st Century.*

The press is one of the leading independent publishers of haiku in the UK.
Since 2013 we have also run a regular IRON Press Festival round the harbour in our native Cullercoats.
IRON in the Soul, our third festival, took place in Summer 2017.
Plans are afoot for a 2019 festival.

We are delighted to be a part of Inpress Ltd, which was set up by Arts Council England to support independent literary publishers.
Go to our website (www.ironpress.co.uk) for full details of our titles and activities.